# MURDER AT ST. GEORGE'S CHURCH

# COPYRIGHT

*THIS BOOK USES BRITISH SPELLING*

# CHAPTER ONE

"*L*ady Gold, will you do me the honour of being my wife?"

Ginger stared down at the handsome man as he risked a grass stain on his knee. He looked up with hopeful hazel eyes.

For the briefest of moments, they became Basil Reed's eyes—his face, his earnest gaze—before Captain William Beale's face returned. Ginger and the Canadian naval captain had met through Ginger's friend Reverend Oliver Hill shortly after Basil had left for his furlough of undetermined length. She'd heard from Basil only once in the six weeks he'd been gone, a letter that let her know that he'd arrived in Cape Town safely, but not much more.

"Ginger?" the captain prompted. The hope in his eyes had made way for worry.

The setting for the marriage proposal, the flower garden at St. George's Church, was quaint. Oliver Hill was to be married tomorrow, and she and the captain had arrived early to help set up and decorate. Captain Beale—a pleasant-looking man with a ready smile, and untameable wavy hair—had been quite determined to steer her away from the sanctuary to get her alone in the garden. Now Ginger knew why.

"Lady Gold?" Captain Beale's voice had taken on a distinct tinge of distress. "An answer would be nice."

"I'm sorry. It's just . . . this is so unexpected. I didn't realise you'd been considering marriage. We've only just met."

"It's been a glorious month, Ginger. Enough for me to know I want to spend the rest of my life with you."

Ginger's heart spat and sputtered. William Beale was a wonderful man who would make a fine husband. Yet—

William Beale sighed. "Shall I get up off my knee?"

"Oh, William! I really need some time to think about it."

William shifted up off the ground and brushed grass from his trousers. "I suppose that is better than a firm 'no.'"

"I'm sorry—"

"No need to apologise, my dear." William took her hands and cupped them with both of his. "It was presumptuous of me to spring this on you without proper warning. Might I ask again in two weeks?"

A HORSE and carriage delivering pink and white roses had parked in front of the church.

"The floral arrangements are here," Ginger said,

thankful for a task that gave her and William something to do other than soak in the pool of ill ease they suddenly found themselves in. How had Ginger not seen that proposal coming? Surely, she hadn't been emitting marital signals—*had she?* William was a good man, handsome, and monied, so she didn't have to worry about his motivations in that regard. So what was it that kept her from saying yes?

*Basil Reed.*

Blast that man!

Well, the good chief inspector had had his chance. How was she to know if he would even return to London? Perhaps the exotically scented air of sun-drenched South Africa was the cure for all that ailed him. Including Ginger!

He wasn't here, and William was. That should tell her something.

"They're beautiful!" Ginger said as the deliverymen carried the flowers inside.

"Let me help," William offered as he made long, quick strides towards the carriage, deftly keeping a full six feet between himself and the rear of the horse.

Ginger had volunteered to oversee the flower order and delivery. She wished the happy couple tremendous goodwill and wanted to do what she could to make their day the best.

St. George's Church was an eighteenth-century structure built of limestone. A square turret edged with castle-like crenellations rose above the end of the sanctuary. The building was simple but beautiful, and Ginger imagined a great many wedding ceremonies had taken place here over the centuries.

Inside, St. George's was a modest sanctuary with rows of wooden pews facing the intricate stained-glass window —vibrant reds, yellows, and blues—which made up images of Jesus and the saints. A narrow wooden door on the far left of the vestry led to the balcony above. The free-standing pipe organ, situated at the back of the balcony, was currently being played by Mrs. Esme Edwards. Ginger couldn't help but wince. Here was a lady who really wanted to be a good musician but didn't actually have the talent. Oliver was too kindhearted to turn her away, but Ginger worried a less compassionate parishioner might not be so gracious.

Someone such as the organist's husband and choir director, Mr. Theodore Edwards, who was there to prepare for the forthcoming choir rehearsal. A more unsuitable couple couldn't be found at St. George's. Mr. Edwards was a fairly attractive man in his forties, having kept his trim physique and most of his hair. His wife didn't fare quite as well with age, her figure having swelled and her hair turning a noticeable salt and pepper. Mr. Edwards had eyes for the fairer sex, but not a kind word left for his wife. She wore her contempt for her husband like a shield. They were the cautionary tale all couples walking the aisle to a "happily ever after" should heed.

A small pit of worry spun in Ginger's stomach. Privately, she held deep concerns for Oliver and his choice of bride. Not that they weren't both wonderful people, but she felt the marriage plans had come on too suddenly, and she couldn't help but feel they were ill-suited for long-term bliss. She wished she could say something, but she knew neither party was open to hearing any sort of dissent, and now with the wedding only a day away, it was too late.

Mr. Edwards lifted his chin to the back of the nave. "Esme! Are you stomping on the keys?"

Mrs. Edwards' response was to pound even louder with an added wrong note.

William shared a startled look with Ginger. "Oh, my."

Mr. Edwards, seemingly unaware that he and his wife were being observed, disappeared through the vestry door that opened to steps that led to the balcony, and charged towards the organ loft. In moments, he stood face-to-face with his wife exchanging words that Ginger didn't wish to overhear.

"Oh, my," William repeated.

READY TO BE HUNG and strung, roses and bunches of tiny white baby's breath filled the entrance area.

"Where did Felicia go?" Ginger said, more to herself than the captain. "She's supposed to help me decorate."

"I'm afraid I don't know," William answered.

Ginger walked toward the exterior door that was a shortcut to the parish hall. "I believe all the fun is happening in the kitchen."

Angry voices travelled along the spring breeze. Ginger could make out a man and woman having words. The man was Mr. Edwards, again, but the woman was too tall to be his wife. Ginger squinted and made out the face of Miss Marjorie Bertram. Soon Miss Bertram disappeared around the corner, and Mr. Edwards walked heavily in their direction, stopping short when he saw he wasn't alone.

"Mr. Edwards," Ginger said. "Is everything all right?"

Theo Edwards pasted a smile over his scowl. "Simply splendid." Noting Ginger's doubtful frown, he added, "Oh, you heard that." His gaze shifted to the floor. "Just a disagreement on hymn choice."

"Doesn't the bride choose the hymns?" Ginger asked.

Theo Edwards grabbed the lifeline Ginger had unintentionally thrown to him. "Yes, yes, that's what I was saying to Miss Bertram. It's up to the bride, now if you'll excuse me, I—" Mr. Edwards darted off before finishing his sentence.

"Odd fellow," William said. "Not well liked, I gather."

"He seems friendly enough to me," Ginger said with a shrug. "Quite a competent choir director. Certainly having an off day, I'd say."

As Ginger had expected, Felicia was in the kitchen, a simply designed but efficient room for creating large quantities of food and baking—an abundance of which covered every available counter and tabletop surface. Mrs. Davies—the spry, grey-haired church secretary—and the slim and pretty Matilda Hanson—a former resident of Hartigan House—bustled about with aprons on and flour in their hair as they baked yet another batch of shortbread.

"There you are, Felicia," Ginger said brightly. "The roses have arrived."

"Oh, Ginger," Felicia said. "Look at all these lovely cakes! An angel cake, a Dundee, a French gateau. The coconut macaroons are simply smashing!"

Felicia Gold had dark hair cut in a trendy bob and wore a white and violet afternoon frock of printed chiffon, with a one-sided material tie. A crossed bodice trimmed with open stitching joined a flared skirt, which had a butterfly bow on the hip. Almost a decade younger than Ginger, not even twenty-two, Felicia had the playful energy to show for it. There was a smudge of flour on the chin of her teardrop face, which Ginger wiped off with her handkerchief.

"Thank you, Ginger," Felicia said. "Mrs. Davies was so kind to allow me to test a sample. It's frightfully delicious!"

"It smells heavenly," Ginger said. "So nice of you, Mrs. Davies. I hope my sister-in-law hasn't been getting underfoot."

"Not at all," Mrs. Davies said, though Ginger wasn't sure if she was being completely honest. Mrs. Davies, seeing William at Ginger's side, said, "Hello, Captain Beale."

William, hat in hand, bowed his head. "Good day, Mrs. Davies, Miss Hanson, and Miss Gold."

"Come now, Felicia," Ginger beckoned. "We've got work to do." Just as they approached the kitchen door, a young lady bounded through. Ginger recognised her as Miss Bertram, also a choir member and the lady who'd supposedly been arguing with Theo Edwards about hymn choice. From the redness evident in Miss Bertram's eyes, Ginger was even more inclined to disbelieve Mr. Edwards' story.

"Miss Bertram," Ginger said. "Is everything all right?"

"Oh yes, Lady Gold," she said with a slight dip to her knees, a habit formed from when Miss Bertram worked in service. "Just chopping onions." She hurried to Mrs. Davies' side. "Put me to work, Mrs. Davies."

ONCE THEY WERE out of earshot, Ginger said, "I didn't see any onions out. The kitchen smelt sweet not savoury." Whatever had brought Miss Bertram to tears, it wasn't something that had happened whilst baking shortbread.

"A personal matter, I suppose," William said. His voice had lost its normal chipper ring. A failed proposal could do that, Ginger thought. Interestingly, she'd completely forgotten about the affair with just a simple distraction. That didn't necessarily mean she should decline his offer. Experience had trained Ginger to keep heart and mystery matters separated in her mind, and Miss Bertram's lie, along with Theo Edwards' lie, was indeed a mystery, albeit a minor one. Her American friend, Haley Higgins, would be quick to tell her that this was none of her business.

Felicia let out a gasp of exhilaration on seeing the mass of pink and white roses. "This sanctuary is going to be so beautiful when we've finished."

"It is indeed, miss." The voice came from behind them,

and was that of a young lady—Anna Howard, another choir member—with a broom in her hand. These ladies were a helpful bunch.

"Miss Howard," Ginger said. "I see you've come prepared."

"Dust and debris from the floral arrangements shall need sweeping up once we have them hung." She sighed. "I do envy the bride." She looked up at Ginger, William, and Felicia with a shocked look, as if she hadn't meant to say that last bit aloud. Her face grew crimson enough to compete with Oliver on a normal day. "I mean," she rushed to explain, "what shall us single ladies do now that we don't have an unmarried vicar to gossip about." She giggled awkwardly and picked up a bundle of roses, effectively hiding her face.

Ginger and Felicia shared a commiserative glance.

They combined roses, white with pink, added sprigs of baby's breath, and tied small bouquets with long strands of white ribbon. Each bunch was attached to the end of the aisle-facing pews. William worked on setting up candelabra stands, and Miss Howard opened a box of fresh unlit candles.

When they had finished, they stood at the back of the sanctuary to admire the results.

"The bride is sure to love it," Ginger declared.

"Oh, dear."

The trio turned on their heels at the sound of the lady's voice. The *bride's* voice.

Ginger smiled warmly. "Hello, Mary."

Mary Blythe, a quiet dentist's receptionist, was Oliver

Hill's choice for a bride. She was pretty in a wholesome way, with clear skin and round eyes. Her hair was short and tucked in under her yellow felt cloche hat. She stared beyond Ginger to the beautiful floral display.

"What do you think?" Ginger asked.

Her dainty hand flew to her mouth. "I think I'm going to be sick."

# CHAPTER TWO

As Ginger watched Mary Blythe disappear down the passage, her mind went to the afternoon of Oliver and Mary's engagement party which Ginger had hosted in her back garden a month ago. It had been a lovely spring day with Clement's handiwork evident in the recent bloom of the flower garden, and everything trim and tidy. Mrs. Beasley had provided the party with teacakes and finger sandwiches of every sort, and the tea was perfectly brewed.

Hand in hand, Oliver and Mary had approached her, thanking her for the millionth time.

"Dearest Ginger," Oliver started. "Your generosity knows no bounds. This is simply wonderful."

"Oh, you put me on too high a pedestal," Ginger said with a light laugh. "I've not lifted a finger to help."

"Well, we must thank your staff then," Oliver said.

Mary remained quiet at his side, smiling as a newly engaged lady is bound to, but something wasn't quite right. Ginger watched her guest of honour with interest. It was the eyes. They lacked a certain sparkle that normally came with the anticipation of a bride-to-be's new life with the man she loved. Once again, the knotted thread of worry tightened in Ginger's chest. She wondered at Oliver's choice of a bride. He had been unofficially commissioned by the bishop to find a wife in order to thwart the distraction he'd been causing to the young single ladies in his parish. Had he chosen too quickly?

If Oliver was bearing any regrets, he was hiding it well.

Ginger scanned the faces of the guests, hoping to find that everyone was enjoying themselves. She didn't know all the attendees, mostly just the choir members she'd met after recently joining the singing group. The Edwards family was huddled to one side; Mr. Cecil Piper—a youthful man who had early hereditary baldness and a need for spectacles—was engaged in conversation with a man Ginger didn't know; Miss Howard and Miss Bertram had arrived late, not together, apparently, just an untimely coincidence. They made this quite clear as they split up to mingle. Ginger got the feeling that the two girls didn't care for one another.

Matilda Hanson and Felicia had finished a conversation, and Felicia left to join Ginger's visiting half-sister, Louisa. Matilda's eyes searched the small crowd of guests until they locked on the person she was looking for. Ginger followed her gaze and was startled to find it had landed on Oliver. The happy countenance Matilda had worn whilst conversing with Felicia changed as she studied the reverend. Her eyes darkened, looking forlorn and rather heartsick.

Oh, mercy.

"Beale, old chum," Oliver suddenly called out. "Over here."

Stepping through the gathering came a slender man with warm eyes and a large grin. "Hill, you old dog," the man said, slapping Oliver on the back. "You're finally tying the knot, eh?"

Oliver laughed. "Something you should consider someday, my friend. So glad you could make it!" Oliver pulled Mary into the circle. "Mary, this is my good friend Captain William Beale. Beale, my fiancée, Miss Blythe."

William extended a hand. "It's a privilege to meet you, Miss Blythe. May I extend my congratulations. You've found an exemplary man in Oliver." He pivoted to include Ginger. "Oliver, please don't delay in introducing me to this beautiful lady."

"Do forgive me. Ginger, meet my good friend, Captain William Beale. Beale, this is Lady Gold, the owner of this lovely house, and hostess of our party. Ginger, this is my good friend Captain William Beale. We met during the war."

"He was my chaplain," Captain Beale explained. "And a grand job he did!"

Oliver grew pink at the praise. "I was glad to serve the king."

"How do you do, Captain?" Ginger said as she extended a white-gloved hand. Her pale-yellow spring frock fluttered in the breeze. It had a stylish pleat in the skirt, a matching crepe scarf that hung over her left shoulder, and on her head was a playful printed cloche garnished with a cluster of purple grapes, pulled low, leaving the tips of her red bob curled up against her cheeks.

"My day has improved tremendously," William said with a grin. "Would you be willing to take a turn about the garden with me?"

Ginger found the gentleman to be quite agreeable, even if his thick wavy hair proved to be rogue.

"It would be my pleasure. If you don't mind my little Boston Terrier joining us," she added.

The captain laughed. "I couldn't think of a better chaperone."

Ginger commanded Boss to follow at her heel as they began their stroll. "Your accent isn't English, Captain Beale," Ginger said. "Canadian?"

"Very good. The Brits usually mistake me for American, and the Americans mistake me for a Brit!"

Ginger chuckled. "I've only been to Canada once, on a business trip with my father when I was younger. We lived in Boston at the time. Montreal is a lovely city, the most like a European city in all of North America. Imagine my surprise when I learned later on that most Canadians spoke English rather than French."

"It's a common mistake," Captain Beale said with a smile.

"What brings you to London?" Ginger asked. She almost missed the Captain's answer because she caught sight of the

Edwards family looking tense as if they were having a quarrel. Mr. Edwards' sister, Miss Catherine Edwards, was wearing a tight expression and looked displeased. She was ignoring the harsh words being spoken between husband and wife, her eyes on Mr. Piper. Mr. Piper, in turn, seemed to steadfastly keep his gaze *away* from Catherine, though he didn't appear to be looking at anything else.

"I promised myself I'd return to Europe after the war to see it in peacetime," Captain Beale was saying. "To visit my friends here." He added more solemnly. "Those who are still alive."

Ginger reined in her attention in time to respond. "Like Oliver?"

"Wonderful fellow. His spiritual advice and example helped me to keep my hope up as well as my head."

Louisa's laughter bubbled from her position in the middle of the garden and her American accent was clearly heard by all. "In America we call this a *yard*, and we don't bother naming our *houses*. It's not like they can come if called! But I do love London. It's so old and quaint!" Louisa didn't even blush. She loved being the centre of attention and was entirely blind to how offensive she could be.

"Who's that lovely world traveller?" Captain Beale asked with a crooked grin.

"That would be my sister, Louisa."

"Sister? But you're English! And you look nothing alike."

"I am English, but my father moved us to Boston when

I was eight, to marry an American. Louisa came along a couple of years later."

Ginger noticed she wasn't the only one whose gaze had turned to Louisa. Mr. Piper had spared a glance over his spectacles. Oliver took a moment to stare over Mary's head. Haley, who was currently huddled in a conversation with Matilda, smiled. Felicia rolled her eyes. Mrs. Edwards couldn't be bothered with the antics of a silly girl, but Mr. Edwards' gaze lingered in a disconcerting fashion. Catherine Edwards watched her brother and scowled.

"I think I should mingle with the guests, Captain Beale," Ginger said politely.

"Of course," the captain said. "How rude of me to hog the lovely hostess all to myself!"

Ginger smiled graciously. "I'm sure no one even noticed."

Instead of stepping away, the captain took a step closer. "I plan to be in London for some time. Would you allow me to pay you a visit?"

Ginger stilled. Would she?

Besides her husband Daniel, Lord Gold, when he was alive, Chief Inspector Basil Reed was the only man she'd considered stepping out with. Oh, she flirted harmlessly with men at social events, but never to the point that she'd allow them to think there was something to be had between them beyond the conversation they were sharing.

She'd even decided recently that she could remain single. She had money and family and good friends. Her emotional needs were attended to. She found a great sense of gratification working with Oliver and their charity the Child Wellness Project. Plus, she enjoyed her work running Feathers & Flair, as well as the small side private investigation jobs she was hired for on occasion.

However, the captain was a charming man and would be a perfectly fine companion for the time he planned to stay in the city. Why not have a little fun? She forced the image of Basil Reed's face from her mind.

"I'd be delighted."

# CHAPTER THREE

Mary Blythe did look a bit green.

"Perhaps you should sit down," Ginger said as she gently guided the bride-to-be past the roses and into a pew.

Mary leaned forward to put her head between her legs. Her hand went to her hat, and for a second, Ginger feared she was going to rip it off to capture her vomit.

"Do you need to lie down? I believe there's a settee in Oliver's office."

"No, I'm fine." Mary lifted her head and pressed a folded handkerchief on her damp forehead. "I wanted to elope," she confessed. "I have a nervous stomach and hate being the centre of attention."

Oh, mercy.

"You'll be so happy once it's over," Ginger said. "Try to think about that instead. Are you going on a wedding journey?"

"Oh, Lord." Mary bounded out of the pew and ran out of the sanctuary, turning in the direction of the ladies.

"She must really love Reverend Hill," Felicia said. "Clearly, she's afraid of crowds."

She's afraid of *something*, Ginger thought, regretting that she had brought up the wedding night. The whole idea of physical intimacy could be overwhelming when one was young and inexperienced. Ginger remembered her first night with Daniel—

"Ginger?"

Ginger snapped out of her reverie. "Yes, Felicia?"

"Shall we go?"

"Yes, but I'd like to say hello to Oliver first," Ginger said. She was surprised that he hadn't made an appearance. Oh dear. She hoped he didn't have cold feet.

"We'll wait for you at your motorcar," William added. Ginger nodded, relieved that William hadn't insisted on coming with her to speak to Oliver. He'd once confessed to feeling envious of Ginger's friendship with his old friend, and if Oliver hadn't been engaged to be married, William said he might've felt threatened.

Even so, Ginger questioned William's possessiveness but extended grace for his behaviour. He was likely still feeling the pinch of her rejection of his proposal and was silently licking his wounds.

The door to Oliver's office was closed, and Ginger knocked. "Oliver? It's Ginger."

Her announcement was met with the shuffling sound of Oliver's chair being scraped across the floor. He flung the door open, eyes darting down the hall past Ginger, then waved her in. His actions reminded her of more than one situation during the war when Ginger had made clandestine assignations, though Oliver was far too animated to be mistaken for a true secret service man.

"Oliver? Is everything all right?" Ginger was starting to feel like a parrot with the question.

"Yes, no, I don't know!" Oliver folded his long legs and collapsed into his chair. He ran a hand over his red curls, which were escaping the oil that usually restrained them.

Ginger took the chair facing his desk. "Do you have cold feet? It's quite normal if you do."

"That must be it. Cold feet. Yes. Mary, she's a sweet girl. She's so nervous; I can't help but wonder if she wants to go through with it. I've given her an option to not go through with it, but she insists she wants to marry me."

"Do you want to marry her?"

"Ginger, the wedding is in two days!"

"It's not too late. Not until you say, 'I do.'"

Oliver startled her with a hearty, forced laugh. His behaviour was so uncharacteristic that Ginger felt genuinely alarmed.

"Of course, it's too late," Oliver said once he regained control of his emotions. "I asked her to marry me, and she said yes. I can't renege on my offer. Besides, can you imagine the uproar it would cause in the diocese? They'd remove me from St. George's faster than, than, than—whatever goes fast!"

Ginger had worried this would happen. Intuitively, she had doubted this union was right for Oliver, but at the time when she could have mentioned it, Oliver had refused to bring her into his confidence. "Oliver, I think you need to take a couple of deep breaths. I'll get us some tea. Would you like some tea?"

"No, I've already had a pot of it. I'm wearing out the carpet to the loo."

"Yes, right. Well, then, let's talk about Mary. Tell me all the things you love about her."

"She's sweet," he repeated. "Gentle, kind, and makes a great beef brisket."

"There you go," Ginger said. "All the makings of a great wife."

"She didn't want a church wedding," Oliver said. "Can you imagine, a vicar of the Church of England *eloping*?"

"It seems to me she just doesn't want a big wedding."

"You're right, Ginger. See? If I were a loving husband, I would've understood her need. Instead, I bent to the expectation of my parishioners. They would run me out of London if I failed to invite them."

"You were just doing what you felt was best. Your parishioners matter, and Mary matters. As a vicar's wife, she must understand that she'll be in the spotlight now."

"Exactly!" Oliver said brightly. In the next moment his expression crumpled "Oh, Lord, I've made a terrible mistake."

"Oliver, Mary shall adjust. She loves you. And she's young. You must give her time."

"Yes, of course, you're right. I don't know what's wrong with me, Ginger. I'm a complete wreck. I've never felt so . . . out of my depth before."

"You shall be fine, Oliver, and so shall Mary. A month from now, this shall all be a distant memory."

Oliver sighed. "Thank you, Ginger. You are a terrific friend."

Ginger smiled. "As are you to me." She stood, and Oliver followed suit. "William and Felicia are waiting for me. I'll see you tonight."

"Tonight? Right. The choir rehearsal. Mary wants to drop in to listen."

"How nice." Ginger had joined the choir ensemble along with Felicia, Louisa, and a reluctant Haley, whom she'd also convinced to join. Haley preferred work as a junior pathologist to hymn singing, but, as Ginger had argued, one couldn't spend all one's time with the dead.

# CHAPTER FOUR

Ginger parked her polished ivory Crossley motorcar in front of the Savoy Hotel, a luxury hotel situated in Westminster. William, sitting on the luxurious red leather seat beside her, turned expectantly. Ginger couldn't ignore the fact that Felicia was sitting in the back seat, observing. She glanced over her shoulder with a meaningful look, and Felicia snapped to attention.

"Oh, yes," she said, then quickly opened the door and slid out. She had the good sense to look interested in something on the street, giving Ginger and William room for a private conversation.

"William," Ginger began.

William held up a palm. "It's okay. We needn't talk about it. Let's just pretend it didn't happen, and when you're ready, you can give me some kind of signal."

"A signal?"

"Yes. You can whistle *God Save the King*."

Ginger protested, "I can't whistle," though it wasn't strictly true. With two fingers, she could whistle loud enough to challenge a steam engine, but when it came to whistling a tune, she was capable of nothing but a puff of air.

"Can't whistle, eh?" William said, his lips tugging into a smile. "Well then, how about you pull on your right ear?"

Ginger worried she might do something like that without the intended meaning attached.

"How about I just say, "Please ask me again.""

William's eyes sparkled with hope. "Splendid! Clear and simple. That's what I admire about you, Ginger."

"I'm clear and *simple*?"

"No!" Mortification flashed across the captain's face. "I mean, you are straightforward and unpretentious. What you see is what you get." William's expression grew pinched. "Oh dear, I'm making a mess of things."

"It's fine, William." Ginger patted his arm reassuringly. "I know what you mean. So, I shall see you at the wedding tomorrow?"

"Indeed. Do you wish me to pick you up in a taxicab?"

"I can meet you there. I'll get Clement to drive us. Haley, Felicia, and Ambrosia are coming along as well." Ginger generally preferred driving her own motorcar whenever possible, but when alcohol was involved, as it was sure to be at the reception, Ginger always opted for a taxicab or arranged for Clement to drive.

"Until tomorrow, then," William said. He leaned over to kiss Ginger, and she immediately offered her cheek.

Even though they were in her motorcar, they were still in public.

Felicia took William's place when he left.

"Poor Captain Beale," Felicia said.

Ginger shot her a sideways glance before pulling the Crossley into traffic. "Why do you say that?"

"He's clearly smitten with you, Ginger. I guarantee an offer of marriage is not far off."

Ginger kept her face bland, her eyes not leaving the road in front of her. She changed the subject. "Oliver and Mary are both having a case of the pre-wedding jitters."

"I saw that too," Felicia said. "And don't think I didn't notice that you failed to comment on Captain Beale's intentions towards you."

"Nothing to comment on at the moment," Ginger said breezily.

She drove down Pall Mall past the red-brick Tudor royal residence of St. James's Palace. She passed slower moving horses and carriages and dodged unsuspecting pedestrians. Felicia held onto her hat, but Ginger thought that a bit dramatic since Felicia was safely inside the cab of the motorcar and in no danger of actually losing headwear.

Ginger avoided getting into a minor accident on the sharp turn at Piccadilly, but a strong spin on the steering wheel put her in the path of some broken glass, and the Crossley jerked to a stop.

Felicia had finally had enough.

"Seriously, Ginger!" She stormed out of the motorcar, slamming the door behind her.

Ginger walked around the motorcar and frowned at the deflating tyre.

Felicia glared at her sister-in-law.

"What?" Ginger said innocently. "That wasn't my fault. I can't help it if there is dangerous debris left on the road."

Eventually, Ginger waved down a black taxicab. The ride past Hyde Park and Kensington Gardens was uneventful, and the cab came to a stop in front of the iron gates belonging to Hartigan House, her home in Mallowan Court in South Kensington.

"Made it with my life intact!" Felicia said as she removed herself from the taxicab.

"Oh, please," Ginger said as she paid the cabby. "It was a flat tyre, not a blazing crash."

Ginger's gardener, Clement, was trimming hedges in the front garden with the help of Ginger's ward, Scout Elliot.

Young Scout was the newest member of what Ginger considered her family. A waif she'd initially met onboard the SS *Rosa* on her journey from Boston to Liverpool, Scout had worked in steerage and helped to look after Boss, Ginger's beloved Boston terrier. When Scout had suddenly been left alone in London without kin to care for him, Ginger hadn't hesitated to collect him.

"H-ello, missus!" Scout said as Ginger and Felicia approached. "H-ello, Miss Gold." Ginger was pleased with how Scout worked hard on not dropping his aitches. His front teeth were almost fully grown in, making his face look a little too small for his mouth. Wheat-coloured hair poked out from under his flat cap, which he tipped like a gentleman. Ginger's heart almost burst with a warm maternal-like affection.

"Hello, Scout. I see you're hard at work."

"He is," Clement said, overhearing. "He's a good helper."

Scout's freckled face beamed with pride. Felicia greeted Scout and Clement and walked briskly ahead of Ginger, disappearing inside.

"You didn't bring the Crossley home, madam?" Clement asked.

"I'm afraid we had a little mishap," Ginger said. Clement's jaw sagged with a look of horror.

"Oh, nothing serious," Ginger added quickly. "The tyre blew, and there's a nasty bend in the rim. Such are the hazards of having inflatables, but they are so much nicer to ride on, don't you agree?"

Clement nodded, not looking entirely consoled.

"Would you mind arranging for it to be towed to the garage?" Ginger gave him the address in Piccadilly. "Pippins can assist you with the telephone."

"Certainly, madam," Clement said. He laid his trimming shears down and headed to the servants' entrance at the back of the house.

Ginger entered through the tall wooden door of Hartigan House that led to a vast foyer with glossy marble floors and a grand chandelier that hung from the height of the second floor. An impressive staircase with an emerald runner curved to the landing. Instead of heading to her room upstairs, Ginger detoured past the sitting room to visit the kitchen at the back of the house. The cook, Mrs. Beasley, was busy preparing the evening meal and giving orders to the maids, Grace and Lizzie.

"Grace, put those long arms to work and reach the lard for me from the top shelf." Mrs. Beasley was easily under five feet tall and round like a puff pastry. Salt-and-pepper curls escaped her cook's cap.

"Hello, Mrs. Beasley," Ginger said. "Don't forget we must leave early tonight for the choir rehearsal."

"Madam, I have not forgotten. We will have minestrone soup and shepherd's pie."

"Sounds delicious, Mrs. Beasley." Ginger turned to Lizzie. "Lizzie, where would I find Boss?"

"In front of the fireplace in the sitting room, madam. At least that was where he was when I saw him last."

With Lizzie and Scout around, Ginger never had to worry about Boss being well looked after when she wasn't home. She did miss the little dog when she was out for too long, and went directly to the sitting room to find him. Felicia was there along with Ginger's American half-sister Louisa, and Ambrosia—also known as the Dowager Lady Gold or Grandmother or, with Felicia, Grandmama—who was sitting in the wing chair. Pippins, Ginger's long-time septuagenarian butler, poured afternoon sherries. The skin around his cornflower-blue eyes crinkled deeply with pleasure when he saw Ginger.

"Would you care for a sherry, madam?"

"Thank you, Pips," she said, using the pet name she'd used for the butler since childhood. "That would be delightful."

At the sound of Ginger's voice, Boss' head popped up

from his slumber, and he bounded onto Ginger's lap. "Oh hello, Bossy!" she said as the pup licked her neck. "You missed me, didn't you? I missed you too!"

Ambrosia, sitting poker-straight in her corset, watched in disgust. "Must you let the animal molest you? It's so unbecoming."

"It's not like we're in public, Grandmother."

"I'm here," she stated as if she were public enough.

"Yes, well." Ginger sipped her sherry.

"Hey, sis," Louisa said. "I'm bored." She patted her red, rosebud mouth in a fake yawn to emphasise her point. Her eyebrows were trimmed into narrow, high arches and her lids shadowed in blue. Her dark hair, styled in a fashionable bob and professionally waved, shone under the electric lights. "Surely, there is something fun to do in London? Where do the eligible bachelors hang out?"

There was a moment in time where Ginger had feared that Louisa and Oliver were soft on each other. How could Ginger have explained that one to her stepmother, Sally Hartigan? Louisa had boarded a ship to England without Sally's knowledge, and it had taken numerous telegrams to calm her down, reassuring her that Ginger would take good care of her much younger half-sister.

"I think your mother would kill me if you found a British gentleman friend," Ginger responded. "She's pretty intent on you going back to Boston soon."

"But what about what I want?" Louisa whined. "I like it here."

"You just said you were bored," Felicia countered. "And

I've introduced you to plenty of gentlemen who've fancied you."

Louisa examined the rings on her well-manicured fingers. "I guess I just haven't found one I like."

Ambrosia rolled large round eyes at the banal conversation.

"I have an idea," Ginger said. Her green eyes latched onto Louisa. "You can work for me at Feathers & Flair."

Louisa stared back with dismay. "Are you proposing I be a *shop girl?*"

"Yes. You'd be perfect for the job. You're young, charming, and are well versed in fashion."

"I have money, Ginger. I don't need to *work.*"

"Of course, you don't," Ambrosia stated. "Young society ladies don't have jobs. It's vulgar."

Louisa frowned as the elder Lady Gold looked down her nose. "Ginger has a *job*."

Ambrosia tapped her walking stick onto the floor. "Ginger is a *widow*. She *employs* people to work *for* her."

"Consider it a diversion, Grandmother," Ginger said diplomatically. "She'd be entertained there, which is preferable to being idle here."

Ambrosia grunted, but Ginger could see by the flicker in the elder Lady Gold's blue eyes that she would be agreeable to anything that removed Louisa from Hartigan House.

"It could be fun," Felicia said. "You could try on all the new gowns."

"I can redirect your earnings to the Child Wellness

Project," Ginger said. "Since you have so much money already."

The Child Wellness Project was the charity project that had brought Oliver Hill and Ginger together and ignited their friendship. It provided meals for hungry street children twice a week at St. George's hall.

Louisa's frown deepened. "There's no such thing as too much money. I'll donate half."

"It's a deal. You can start on Monday."

"I think I'll like being a working woman," Louisa said to Felicia importantly. "It says 'independence.'"

"I prefer to offer my time to support good causes," Felicia shot back.

"Has the decorating of St. George's been completed?" Ambrosia asked.

"Yes," Ginger replied. "It looks beautiful. Lovely pink and white rose bouquets—the place smells wonderful. So many candles, we'll have to watch that we don't start a fire."

"*Oooh*," Louisa said. "I can't wait. Though, I don't understand what Oliver sees in Mary Blythe. *I* would've married him, had he asked. It's like he chose unbuttered bread over a piece of rich cream cake."

"Louisa!" Ginger said.

Louisa was unrepentant. "Well, it's true."

"A little humility wouldn't hurt you, young lady," Ambrosia muttered, "though you can't help it, I suppose, being American."

"Mary is a fine choice for Oliver," Ginger said, feeling

like a liar. "She was rather nervous today. I hope she does all right."

"Of course, she's nervous," Ambrosia said. "It's natural to be anxious about getting married."

"She should read Dr. Stopes' book, *Married Love*," Felicia said. "Knowledge is power."

"Felicia!" Ambrosia spouted. "What is wrong with a little polite conversation? Must you always be so crass?"

"Why is married love crass, Grandmama? It's perfectly normal. That's the kind of thinking that keeps womankind in the dark ages."

"Oh child," Ambrosia said with a puff of exasperation. Turning to Ginger, she said, "We must work harder at finding Felicia a husband. She needs taming."

"Grandmama," Felicia said. "Don't talk about me like I'm not in the room. I'll find my own husband, thank you. And *I'll* be the one doing the taming."

Ambrosia pressed her wrinkled lips together with disapproval. Ginger still wasn't used to the elderly lady's newly acquired silver bob hairdo. It had been an impulsive gesture, quite uncharacteristic for her grandmother-in-law, and though Ginger applauded the effort to join the twentieth century, she thought it didn't quite fit somehow.

"I want to read that book," Louisa stated.

Ginger stared at her sister, astounded. "No! Sally would never forgive me. Felicia, do not give that book to Louisa."

"But Ginger, why not?" Louisa pleaded. "I'm almost the same age as Felicia, and she's read it."

"You can read it when the time is right, Louisa," Ginger said. "And that time isn't now."

Louisa huffed, placed her empty sherry glass on the coffee table, and got to her feet. She left the sitting room without saying a word, reminding Ginger of the many temper tantrums performed by Louisa in the past.

Ambrosia put her weight on the silver handle of her walking stick and stood. "Felicia, child, would you escort me upstairs?"

Felicia emptied her drink. She shrugged at Ginger with a look that said, *since when did Ambrosia need help getting up the stairs?* The matriarch was getting older and presumably weaker.

"Where's Langley?" Ginger asked. Langley was Ambrosia's lady's maid.

"She needed time off," Ambrosia answered. "Her mother or father or some relative decided now was a convenient time to die."

*Oh, mercy.* The things Ambrosia was prone to say.

Haley entered just as Ambrosia and Felicia were leaving.

"I sure know how to empty a room," she said as she headed to the sideboard where the drinks were kept. "Something to drink?"

"Yes, please," Ginger said. "Even though I just had a sherry."

"Drinking sherry is like drinking juice," Haley said. "Gin and tonic?"

"Easy on the gin."

Haley mixed the drinks and handed Ginger a glass

before lounging on the settee. She stretched out her stockinged legs and straightened her tweed skirt. Her dark-eyed gaze took in Ginger's stressed expression.

"Hard day?" Haley asked.

"William proposed."

"I see. And I take it you didn't say yes."

"No, I didn't say yes. I didn't say no either. I just wasn't expecting the question. We've only been associating for a month!"

Haley pushed brunette flyaway curls that had escaped her faux-bob behind her ear. "What I'm hearing is Basil Reed's only been gone for a month and a half."

Ginger pierced her American friend with a hard stare. "Basil Reed never even crossed my mind."

Haley's dark brow arched in a symbol of disbelief. She sipped her drink without replying.

"Fine! I thought of him. So? What am I to do about that? He's reprehensible, and . . ." Ginger struggled to find the appropriate adjective.

"And gone," Haley said.

"Yes, and gone!"

Haley sighed. "I'm sorry you're going through this, Ginger. But Basil Reed doesn't deserve you. Perhaps you should open your heart to Captain Beale. He seems like a nice fellow."

"He is nice. And I like him, but . . ."

"You don't love him?"

"No. But perhaps love is overrated. At least the second time around."

"Ginger, you're a rich, independent woman. You don't

need a man around that you don't love."

With impeccable timing, Boss let out a long, low whimper.

"Oh, Bossy. You're right. I have you. I don't need a man."

"That said," Haley continued, "there are different kinds of love. Maybe you'll never love a man again like you loved Daniel, but that doesn't mean you can't find someone who makes you feel loved. Someone who makes you laugh, and with whom you can carry on an intelligent conversation."

"But, Haley," Ginger said with a smile. "I have you for that."

Laughing, Haley responded, "I'm not going to be around forever."

"Oh, mercy. You're not threatening to go back to Boston again, are you?"

"I'm just saying I don't know what I'm going to be doing when I am finished at the medical school."

Ginger took a long pull of her gin and tonic and made a face. "We'll cross that bridge when we get to it, then. You're coming to the choir rehearsal tonight?"

Haley sighed. "I don't know how I let you talk me into joining the choir. I sing like a foghorn."

"You sing fine," Ginger said. "And it's fun. You have to admit it."

"It's interesting."

"Besides, Oliver needs all the support he can get."

"Don't tell me he has cold feet."

"Frozen solid, I'm afraid."

Ginger found Oliver pacing the area in front of the pulpit.

"I'm not used to being on this side of things," he said as she approached.

Ginger patted him on the back. "You only have to do it once."

A stout, older vicar had entered the church and strode down the aisle towards them with quick short strides. He pulled at the white dog collar that fit snugly around a full, soft neck.

"So sorry I'm late, Hill. I promise to be on time tomorrow morning."

"That's quite all right. Mary hasn't arrived."

Oliver explained to Ginger, "Mary and I are meeting with Reverend Markham to discuss a few last-minute matters." He then proceeded to make introductions. "Lady Gold, this is Reverend Markham. Markham, this is my good friend, Lady Gold."

Ginger held out a gloved hand. "Pleased to meet you."

"Likewise," Reverend Markham said with a genuine smile. "I've heard good things about the charitable work you do with Reverend Hill."

Ginger smiled in response. "How kind."

"Reverend Markham is performing the ceremony," Oliver explained.

Theo Edwards' impatient voice interrupted their huddle. "Lady Gold!"

The choir had gathered in their position adjacent to the altar. Ginger was the only person in the small ensemble not there.

"Oh, I'm wanted." She pinched Oliver's arm and whispered encouragingly. "It's all going to be fine."

As an alto, Ginger took her position beside Miss Bertram, Miss Howard, Louisa, and Haley. The soprano section in front of her consisted of Miss Edwards, Felicia, Matilda Hanson and Mrs. Davies. The men, Mr. Robson and Mr. Piper, stood behind them.

Theo motioned to his wife, Esme, sitting before the organ in the loft at the back of the church, and the raucous tones began.

"Can't they do something about that organ?" Louisa muttered.

"Like a new organist, per'aps," Mr. Robson grumbled from behind. "There's nothin' wrong with the organ."

Catherine Edwards glared over her shoulder at the man. "My sister-in-law is a splendid organist."

Theo Edwards jabbed his arms into the air and

shouted, "What on earth are you folks chattering on about?"

Mr. Robson shouted back, "What? Can't 'ear ya over the racket comin' from the balcony."

Theo turned, cupped his mouth, and thundered, "Esme!"

Ginger shared a look with Haley. This could take a while.

Oliver hovered over by the vestry. Ginger smiled when he looked her way, but he didn't smile back. Then Ginger realised it wasn't her Oliver was looking at but Matilda standing in front of her. His eyes were soft and flickered with deep emotion.

*Oh mercy!* Oliver was getting married to the wrong girl!

Matilda Hanson's history was blighted, but God had forgiven her and Oliver never judged. Ginger couldn't believe she'd missed the signals, but when she thought back, she could remember how well Oliver and Matilda had got along, and how sincere their friendship appeared to be.

Matilda had shown emotional restraint, undoubtedly believing she wasn't good enough for the reverend, and Oliver would've had trouble getting the diocese to agree to a union with a "ruined" woman. Mary would've seemed a sensible next choice.

Oh mercy! The happiness of three people was about to be ruined forever!

Ginger could hardly concentrate on the music and was relieved that Mr. Edwards had called for a break after two hymns. However, his reason for halting the rehearsal was unpleasant. He stomped off and grumbled loudly, "This is a disaster," leaving them to stand in their rows without explanation.

"Well, I'm going to see how things are going in the kitchen," Mrs. Davies said, dispersing quickly along with the other choir members. Matilda followed.

Haley, Felicia, and Mr. Robson retired to a pew. Louisa, ever energised, wandered the nave staring at the simple religious art frescos along the walls and admiring the stained glass. Oliver had stepped out of the vestry to peek in on the racket and joined Ginger, who stood in the north transept.

"How's it coming along?" Oliver asked with a note of doubt.

"Not well, I'm afraid." Ginger checked her wristwatch —6:10 p.m.—and hoped the break wouldn't last too long. She was eager to get home to a hot bath and a good book. "Mr. and Mrs. Edwards don't exactly see eye to eye."

Oliver nodded. Ginger thought her friend appeared rather despondent and not at all like a nervous, yet excited, groom should look. "Where did Reverend Markham go?" she asked him.

"He found the choir rehearsal rather unpleasant and asked if he could wait in my office until Mary arrived."

"She's still not here?"

"No. I'm not sure what's keeping her. Something must've come up. At least Reverend Markham is in the office, should she ring."

"I'm sure she has a good reason for being delayed,"

Ginger said. She hoped Mary wasn't about to leave poor Oliver at the altar. Mary had looked like a frightened rabbit that morning.

Then out of the corner of her eye, Ginger saw a blur of colour as a heavy object plunged from the upper balcony.

Louisa screamed.

# CHAPTER SIX

With one knee draped over the back of the pew lay the twisted body of Theo Edwards.

"Oh, good Lord!" Oliver said.

With impeccably bad timing, Mary Blythe chose that moment to arrive.

"Oliver?"

Oliver turned his back to the body in an attempt to block his bride's view of the gruesome spectacle. "Perhaps you could find Reverend Markham. He's in my office."

Mary ignored Oliver's request and walked around him. "Is he . . . dead?"

It was apparent to Ginger that the choir director was indeed dead—his chest was still, his lips blue, and his eyes open and unblinking. Blood trickled down the side of his face. Haley had rushed over and checked for a pulse.

"He's gone," she said grimly.

Louisa lowered herself onto a pew away from the dead man, looking green. "I think I'm going to be sick."

Ginger hurried to her side. "Lower your head towards your knees."

"I don't think that's going to help!" Louisa ripped the spring hat off her head and vomited into it. "Oh, stinkers!" she moaned. "This is so humiliating."

Felicia, who had unfortunately encountered death before, displayed a stronger constitution.

"Felicia, darling," Ginger pleaded. "Can you assist Louisa? Take her to the ladies' room to clean herself up."

Felicia took Louisa's arm as the girl bellowed, "I've never seen a dead person before. The horror will be etched on my eyelids for all time!"

"What's going on here?" Esme's voice echoed through the nave. Then she saw her husband's body gawking sightlessly skyward. A hand flew to her bosom. "Dear Lord!"

Catherine Edwards, having followed her sister-in-law into the nave, fell to her knees. "Theo? *Theo?*" Her voice grew increasingly hysterical. "Is my brother *dead?*"

Ginger rushed to Miss Edwards' aid. "Come now, get on your feet." Catherine's trembling body leaned heavily against Ginger as she moved Catherine to a pew closer to the pulpit and out of sight of the corpse. "Lady Gold, what happened to my brother?"

"It appears that he fell from the balcony. A terrible accident."

Catherine began to sob, and Ginger produced her

handkerchief. "Now, try to calm yourself. I'll see if Mrs. Davies can bring you some tea."

Ginger returned to the huddle. By now Mrs. Davies, Matilda, Reverend Markham, and Mr. Piper had arrived.

"Oh, poor soul," Mrs. Davies said.

"Indeed," Ginger said. "Mrs. Davies, would you mind calling for a doctor and then putting on some tea? I believe we're all going to need a cup."

"Yes, thank you, Lady Gold. I'd be happy to have something useful to do."

"Such a tragedy," Reverend Markham commiserated. "And just before what is meant to be such a happy event.

Mr. Piper only frowned then went to sit beside Catherine Edwards.

"How did he fall?" Oliver asked. "I didn't see."

"I didn't see either," Ginger said. "I only caught sight of him on his way down." She turned to the new widow. "Had he gone up there to see you, Mrs. Edwards?"

"Well, yes." Mrs. Edwards dabbed at her eyes with the corner of a folded white cotton handkerchief, "but then I left him up there." She wailed. "He must've fallen!"

"Yes," Ginger said simply. The fact that he had fallen was evident. "But why? I mean, he wasn't likely to just tumble over the rail for no reason."

"Perhaps he suffered a heart attack," Reverend Markham said.

"Well, this is rot," Mr. Robson said, checking his watch. "The missus 'as beef casserole waiting."

"It's a terrible inconvenience for us all, Mr. Robson," Ginger said doubting the man would catch the sarcasm in her voice. "But we must all remain here until the police arrive."

Haley continued to examine the body. "There's no sign of flushing to indicate heart failure. Usually, the skin turns red from the chest up."

"What are you?" Mr. Robson said snidely. "A doctor?"

"She's a student at the London School of Medicine for Women," Ginger said in Haley's defence. "You're welcome to take over if you have better credentials."

Mr. Robson huffed but backed away.

"Haley?" Ginger prodded.

"He does have a nasty wound on his temple. It's responsible for the blood on his face and on his shirt."

"He must've hit his head on something," Oliver said.

"Yes," Haley said, though Ginger noted her friend didn't sound convinced.

"Is there a problem?" Ginger asked.

Haley's gaze moved from the body to the balcony. "What could he have hit his head on? There's nothing in the way."

"On the edge of the pew, perhaps?" Ginger said.

"A blow to the head from a fall from that height would've resulted in immediate death."

"The heart would've stopped pumping," Ginger filled in.

"Right. Very little blood would've resulted."

"What do you think it means?" Ginger asked.

Haley exhaled and stared back. "I think he was struck before he fell."

Oxygen sucked out of the room for an instant before everyone gasped.

"Are you saying you believe Mr. Edwards' death was intentional?" Ginger asked.

"Yes. He was hit with something, then helped over the rail."

"Murder?" Oliver said in disbelief.

Mrs. Edwards' knees buckled, and Oliver caught her before she hit the floor. "Oh dear. I shouldn't have said that out loud," Oliver said. "Shall I just lay her down?"

"Yes," Haley said. She squatted beside the lady who had fainted and held her wrist between two fingers. "Her pulse is strong. She'll come to, shortly."

Catherine's sobbing had subsided but once again filled the nave with her grief. The way sound travelled in the stone building, it would be impossible not to have heard Haley's pronouncement.

"No one is to leave this church until after the police arrive and say you can go," Ginger announced formally. "Does everyone understand?"

"I was sitting next to Miss Gold the 'ole time," Mr. Robson grumbled. "I 'ardly pushed the man over the railing from 'ere."

"Just as a matter of form, Mr. Robson," Ginger said. She turned to the visiting vicar. "Reverend Markham, would you please ring the police?"

"Of course." The heavyset vicar scurried towards Oliver's office as fast as his short legs could go.

Catherine Edwards' sobbing, though quieter now, filled the silence of the sanctuary.

"Miss Edwards is undone," Ginger whispered to Haley. "Poor thing."

"She could be in shock," Haley said.

Mrs. Davies and Matilda arrived pushing a tea trolley. "We don't normally drink tea in the church, but this is extraordinary."

"Agreed," Oliver said.

Mrs. Davies handed Catherine Edwards a cup before sitting beside the bereaved lady. She placed a soft arm around Miss Edwards' thin shoulders and offered motherly comfort. Matilda poured tea for the rest, starting with Mrs. Edwards who immediately joined her sister-in-law on the pew. Neither of the Edwards women wanted to see the broken body of their husband and brother and kept their gazes on the altar ahead.

Oliver approached Ginger with two cups in hand and gave her one.

"Thank you, Oliver. I've never been in such a need for a cup of tea."

"My pleasure." He cleared his throat, his expression strained. "At the risk of sounding extremely insensitive, what of the wedding on Saturday?"

"I'm afraid you may have to find another church, Oliver. I'm pretty sure the police shall be intruding here for at least a day or so."

"I see."

"Or," Ginger added carefully, "you could postpone it."

"No, Mary is insistent that we marry immediately. She's quite determined. Oh, dear. One can't get married just anywhere, as they do in America. It must be a church, and it's a popular time to wed."

"I'm so sorry this incident has happened. What a horrible event to have associated with your happiest of days."

Oliver's smile was strained. "Lady Gold, the Lord works in mysterious ways."

GINGER HAD EXPECTED Scotland Yard to get involved. A murder at a church was just the kind of thing to get Superintendent Morris excited. She wasn't surprised to see Sergeant Scott approach, a French Furet camera in hand, but her heart nearly stopped at the sight of Basil Reed. He wore a navy-blue cotton suit with a crisp, white shirt and narrow, black silk tie. He removed his trilby hat.

How long had he been back in London? And why had he not sought her out? Her stomach churned with emotion: anger, longing. Relief?

Mostly anger, though Ginger couldn't pinpoint exactly why. Perhaps because he had claimed to love her and then left the country for six weeks without considering how that would affect her.

Basil caught Ginger's eye, his own flashing with surprise and something more personal. Regret? He held her gaze for one long meaningful moment before instructing his team of constables to begin their search for evidence.

"Hello, Chief Inspector Reed," Ginger said tightly

when he turned back to her. "I admit to being surprised to see you."

"You aren't alone in your surprise," Basil said. "Another body and here *you* are."

"Oliver is to be married—was to be married—in two days, and I'm here as a choir member. It appears Superintendent Morris has reinstated you."

"Yes. I've got my credentials back," Basil said. Basil Reed had been suspended for getting involved in a personal case when he'd been ordered to leave it alone. Morris hadn't exiled him, though. Basil had done that to himself.

Ginger was unintentionally blocking the aisle, and Basil had to brush past her to get to the crime scene. The close encounter made her shiver, and she inhaled his musky scent deeply, a move she immediately chastised herself for. She was acquainted with Captain Beale now. Ginger thought of the scent of the captain's slightly sweet aftershave, suddenly aware of how little impact it had on her senses.

She swivelled to follow Basil and stood behind Haley who was in a discussion with Dr. Gupta, the city patholo-gist. Dr. Manu Gupta had been promoted after the former chief pathologist's fall from grace.

"Fresh gash at the temple, which happened before he died," Gupta explained to Basil. "Long enough for blood to spurt with several beats of the heart before breaking his neck on the back of this pew."

"Who witnessed his fall?" Basil asked.

Ginger lifted a hand. "I did. Reverend Hill and I were

standing there," she pointed towards the area near the pulpit. "And from the corner of my eye, I saw Mr. Edwards fall ."

With a short pencil, Basil jotted notes into his pocket notebook.

"I saw the whole thing," Louisa said huskily. She'd recovered from her initial shock and came to stand beside Ginger. She fluttered her eyelids as she spoke to Basil. "I was walking through the nave admiring the art, and I just happened to look up as he folded over the rail."

"And you are?" Basil asked.

Ginger rushed to make introductions. "Chief Inspector Reed, allow me to introduce my younger half-sister, Miss Louisa Hartigan."

"How do you do, Miss Hartigan," he said politely.

Louisa ducked her chin and smiled. "How do you do, Chief Inspector."

Basil's hazel eyes moved from Ginger's face to Louisa and back.

"She takes after her mother," Ginger said, explaining their difference in colouring.

Louisa laid a dainty hand on Basil's suit sleeve. "I was terribly frightened, Chief Inspector. It's such a relief to have a strong, intelligent gentleman to take charge."

Haley coughed into her fist, raising a dark eyebrow.

Basil cleared his throat. "Did you see anyone else up there, Miss Hartigan?"

Louisa hesitated. "I . . . I'm not sure. I think I saw a flash of fabric."

"What colour?" Basil asked. "Do you recall?"

Louisa shook her head. "I'm afraid not. It happened so fast."

"What about you, Miss Higgins?" Basil asked.

"I had my eyes closed, I'm afraid," Haley said.

"She's been putting in extra hours at the lab," Dr. Gupta offered. "One of my best students."

"I just 'eard the whack of his body landing," Mr. Robson grunted.

"I see," Basil said. "Miss Gold?"

"I also only heard the body landing," Felicia answered.

"Who else was present at the time of death?"

Oliver spoke. "Only Lady Gold, myself, Miss Gold, Miss Higgins, Miss Hartigan, and Mr. Robson were in the sanctuary. The others had left the room when Mr. Edwards gave the choir a break."

"And this choir rehearsal was for the benefit of your wedding, Reverend?" Basil asked.

"Yes. To Miss Mary Blythe." Oliver pulled the shivering woman to his side.

"Were you also present, Miss Blythe?"

Oliver answered for her. "No, she arrived late, just after the sad affair."

Basil hummed. "Who else was in the church building?"

Oliver ran through the list of names. "Mrs. Davies, the church secretary; Miss Hanson who helps her in the kitchen; Reverend Markham who was to conduct our wedding."

"*Is* to," Mary interrupted. "*Is* to conduct our wedding."

"Yes, of course. I'm sorry, dear." Oliver cleared his throat with a look of embarrassment and continued. "Mr.

Piper, Miss Bertram, and Miss Howard who are choir members; Mrs. Edwards, the deceased's wife; and Miss Edwards, the deceased's sister."

"Please get them all to take a seat," Basil said.

Sergeant Scott took photographs of the body and the crime scene as one of the constables held and ignited the flash pan. Scott then headed upstairs to the balcony where Theo had toppled over, and the flashes continued.

Basil stood at the front of the church, facing the small assembly Oliver had called to order. Mrs. Edwards looked stunned, and Miss Edwards looked ill—both of them sniffing into handkerchiefs, their chins down. Everyone else watched the inspector with rapt attention.

"No one is to leave the church until I say," he began. "Now, I need to run through Mr. Edwards' last steps."

Miss Edwards filled the sanctuary with a soft moan.

"I know this is difficult, Miss Edwards," Basil said gently. "But I'm afraid it's unavoidable."

"I just can't believe he's gone," she said, dabbing her eyes.

"Mr. Edwards was directing the choir," Basil said as he moved to the chancel area behind the pulpit where the choir had been located. "About here?"

Ginger answered. "That's correct."

"Perhaps, Lady Gold, you could join me and tell me exactly where everyone was standing."

Ginger inhaled, but went to Basil's side, just like old times when they had worked on cases together. She threw her shoulders back, determined to be professional. "From left to right in the back row were Mr. Piper and Mr.

Robson. In front of them were Miss Bertram, Miss Howard, Miss Hartigan, Miss Higgins, and me. Standing in front of us were Miss Edwards, Miss Gold, Miss Hanson, and Mrs. Davies. Mrs. Edwards was on the balcony at the back, playing the organ."

"At what time did Mr. Edwards call for the break?" Basil asked

"At ten past six," Ginger said. "Reverend Hill can confirm that I'd checked my watch for the time."

Basil nodded. "Then what happened?"

Ginger cast a glance at the eager faces sitting in the pews. "Well, if my memory serves me, Miss Higgins, Miss Gold, Miss Hartigan, and Mr. Robson walked to the front pew near the north transept and sat. I joined Reverend Hill on the opposite side. I'm not sure what happened to everyone else."

"What did Mr. Edwards do?"

Ginger pointed to the door leading to the vestry. "He went through that door there."

"And where does that lead?"

Oliver answered. "It leads to the vestry, but there are also stairs to the balcony."

Basil addressed Oliver. "Reverend Hill, is there a room where I can conduct interviews?"

"Certainly. You may use my office," Oliver said. "Is it okay if Mrs. Davies provides tea whilst we wait?"

"Of course."

Basil turned to Ginger and surprised her by asking, "Would you like to join me?"

Ginger had often accompanied Basil in past cases.

Ginger had convinced Basil that suspects, both male and female, would be more open to talking with a female present, and she had, in fact, been correct. When Ginger had started taking work as a private investigator, Basil had asked her to consult with him. Since Ginger had a sound alibi, her involvement wouldn't be considered a conflict.

"I would, thank you."

"Terrific," Basil said with a smile. "But first I'd like to have a look upstairs."

# CHAPTER SEVEN

Ginger followed Basil up the circular stone stairwell.

"So, how long have you been back?" she asked trying, but somehow failing, to keep her voice casual. Her close proximity to this man she once thought she loved had her heart pounding in her chest. She wished to be immune to him by now, but she was anything but. She had to be more diligent than ever to guard her heart and keep her distance.

Basil answered, "One week."

"I see." One week. A whole seven days. Ginger wondered how long it would've been before she would've seen Basil if it hadn't been for this tragedy?

Basil waited at the top and extended his hand. Ginger held the rail firmly and didn't need the help, but it was a gentlemanly gesture, and her breeding compelled her to accept.

"Not necessary, but thank you," Ginger said.

Basil was slow to let her hand go. "I would've rung you soon," he said quietly, answering her unspoken question.

"No need." She stepped around him towards Sergeant Scott, hoping Basil couldn't see how her heart had lodged itself in her throat.

Basil resumed his investigative professionalism. "What have you found, Scott?"

"Bloodstain on the floor, sir, and on the rail."

Basil examined the red smear on the white stucco surface. Ginger's gaze travelled to the nave below. The ambulance team had arrived. Dr. Gupta had left instructions with Haley, and she was standing with the team overseeing the removal of the body.

"Murder weapon?" Basil asked. Sergeant Scott shook his head. "I've scoured the balcony, sir, under every seat, and in every nook and cranny."

Ginger walked towards the organ loft. Basil followed her through the narrow walkway. She kept her head held high but knowing that Basil was watching her from behind made her pulse soar. She hoped the lines on the back of her stockings were straight!

Tucked into a shallow stone alcove, was a small free-standing organ with a series of tin pipes of various sizes jutting out from the top of a dark mahogany console. The original instrument had been much larger, but when the church needed money to keep up the older building, it was sold. As far as Ginger was concerned, this smaller version was more than loud enough.

"If Mrs. Edwards killed her husband," Basil said, "she might've followed him after he spoke to her."

"I witnessed an argument earlier between the two of them," Ginger said.

Basil stilled. "Is that so? Did you hear what it was about?"

"No. But she wasn't afraid to push back. When Mr. Edwards yelled later about her organ-playing skills, she just pounded the keys harder."

"So, not a case of wedded bliss, then?" Basil said.

Ginger ran her fingers over the ivory keys, not making a sound. "I dare say, it wasn't."

"Mrs. Edwards had opportunity, but until we find the murder weapon, we don't have means," Basil said.

"What of motive?" Ginger asked.

"It wouldn't be the first time a disgruntled wife killed her husband."

"Yes, but if spousal frustration were all it took for a murder, then half the married population would be dead by now, I suspect."

Basil rubbed the back of his neck as he conceded. "And the other half hanged."

OLIVER HELPED BASIL and Ginger get set up for the forthcoming interviews in his office. The room was sparse with an ornate desk and well-used leather chair, and sturdy wooden shelves stocked with books on church history, Bible study manuals, concordances, and other texts used for sermon creation. Ginger knew from previous visits that the arched window in the exterior stone wall looked out on a tall hedge that blocked the view of the neighbours. A small fire burned in the hearth keeping the space warm.

"Mrs. Davies shall bring some tea shortly," the vicar said. "She and Miss Hanson are just settling the others in the hall."

"Thank you, Oliver," Ginger said with a smile. She could only imagine the inner turmoil her friend was suppressing to be civil to them. "That would be lovely. Would you mind if I make a quick telephone call?"

"Not at all."

"Please ask Mrs. Edwards and Miss Edwards to come in," Basil said. "Then the ladies shall be free to go."

Ginger picked up the candlestick telephone, cast a glance at Basil, and then asked the operator to connect her to the Savoy Hotel.

"Please let Captain William Beale know I shall be delayed," she started, but before the desk clerk could record the message, he informed her that the captain just happened to be walking by. She heard him call William over.

Another quick glance at Basil found him staring at her unabashedly. She turned her back in a vain effort for privacy.

"Yes, hello, William?"

William seemed surprised but pleased with the call. Ginger hadn't realised just how well the captain's voice travelled. It came loudly and clearly through the receiver Ginger held to her ear, and she had no doubt Basil could hear everything.

"Is everything fine?" the captain asked.

"Yes, everything is fine," she said.

"Is the rehearsal over? How did it go?"

"Well, not good. In fact, the reason I'm calling is to let you know that I've suffered an unpreventable delay. You might hear about an incident at St. George's, and I didn't want you to worry."

"Oh, dear. What happened?"

"Sadly, a man died under suspicious circumstances. I can't get into it now. Scotland Yard is here."

"Superintendent Morris is with you?"

Ginger's gaze darted to Basil who still had not looked away.

"No, not Morris. It's Chief Inspector Reed."

"Oh. He's back?"

"Yes."

Ginger had had one glass of red wine too many one evening over dinner and had confided in the captain about her involvement with Basil Reed and how he'd left her in a lurch. William had called Basil a lout and a cad, and even in her slight state of inebriation, Ginger knew she'd made an error of judgment by talking to him. "He's not so bad," Ginger had said defensively. "For a cad," she added lightly, bringing the hoped-for smile to William's face.

"Nonetheless," the captain had said. "I hope to never meet the man."

Ginger could feel the frost of William's displeasure through the telephone line.

"Do give him my regards," he said coolly.

"Hmm."

"Shall I pick you up? I can hire a motorcar?"

"I'll take a taxicab."

"Are you sure?"

Ginger was *sure* William didn't want her having a lift home with Basil Reed.

"Haley, Felicia, and Louisa are here with me," she said. "We'll share."

"Very well. Am I to assume there's no wedding this weekend?"

"Yes. Now, I must go. Bye, William."

"Bye, darling. Do be careful."

Ginger returned the receiver, took her seat, and smoothed out her skirt, all without looking Basil in the eye. His relentless staring was unnerving. She finally gave in and looked up.

"Darling?" he said without expression.

"Not that it's any of your business," Ginger said defensively, "but I've been stepping out with a fine gentleman. A captain in the Royal Canadian Navy. A friend of Oliver's, actually. They met during the war when Oliver was a naval chaplain." She locked onto Basil's gaze with a challenging glare. "*He* knows what he wants."

Basil returned, "*I* know what I want."

"Oh, and what's that?"

"You."

*Oh, mercy!*

Ginger had learned to control her expressions and emotions during her time working on missions with the British Secret Service in the war and hoped she hadn't got out of practice. She stared unflinchingly at Basil. "It's too—"

"Chief Inspector Reed, Lady Gold," Oliver said as he led the two Edwards ladies into his office. "Mrs. Edwards and Miss Edwards to see you."

Basil's eyes stayed on Ginger for one heart-thudding moment before he straightened his collar and nodded at Oliver. "Yes, thank you, Reverend."

# CHAPTER EIGHT

*M*rs. Edwards and Miss Edwards sat facing Basil who was at Oliver's desk. Ginger remained in the third chair closer to the window. The newly bereaved women held hands in a mutual show of comfort and possibly, Ginger thought, solidarity.

The emotionally stronger of the two, Mrs. Edwards, sat tall, shoulders back, with her wide-brimmed spring hat firmly on her head. She put forth her British stiff upper lip. Catherine's constitution was of the weaker sort, her bones appearing loose as she collapsed in on herself.

"Miss Edwards and Theo were very close," Mrs. Edwards explained. "I fear my sister-in-law is unable to bear the trauma. I really should get her home."

"I understand," Basil said. "We can postpone this until tomorrow or the next day. Give me your home addresses, and I'll call on you after you've had time to rest."

"Miss Edwards lives with me," Mrs. Edwards said after

reciting her street and house number. "I'll be sure to have a pot of tea ready."

Once the Edwards ladies had left, Basil said, "Since you knew the victim, can you think of any reason someone might want to kill him? Especially here, in the church?"

Ginger had been turning that question over in her head ever since the murder had happened.

"Not off the top of my head," she said.

"Money? Did he owe money to anyone, was he embezzling from the church?"

"I'm unaware of Mr. Edwards' business practices, but I'm certain he wasn't involved professionally with any of the choir members. As for embezzlement, Oliver would've confided in me, had he felt concerned. Besides, Mr. Edwards had nothing to do with the church's accounting."

"He was a married man, but not happily?"

"No," Ginger answered. "Despite Mrs. Edwards' show of grief, I've never seen the two of them exchange a civil word."

"Would you say that Mr. Edwards had been an attractive man?"

"I think many ladies may have found him to be."

"I see." Basil referred to his notes. "Would you mind bringing in Miss Bertram and Miss Howard?"

In normal circumstances, Ginger would joke about not being Basil's secretary, and Basil would tease her about not being necessary to the interview. This time Ginger left without complaint to round up the younger choir members, guiding Miss Bertram in first and asking Miss Howard to wait out in the passageway.

Miss Marjorie Bertram's fine-boned hands were clasped loosely on her lap, and her slender ankles crossed. Her brunette hair was cut short with fashionable finger waves pinned off an attractive face.

"Miss Bertram, how well did you know Mr. Edwards?" Basil asked.

"He was the choir director. I was in the choir."

"Did you ever have reason to meet outside of the choir?"

"I'm not sure what you're getting at, Chief Inspector?"

"Was Mr. Edwards overly friendly with the younger lot?"

Ginger shot Basil a look. He was fishing for motive. The way Miss Bertram started fidgeting with her gloves, Ginger thought Basil might've landed on one.

Her mind went to the engagement party and how Mr. Edwards had watched Louisa, and then to the argument she'd witnessed between him and Miss Bertram.

Miss Bertram snorted. "Mr. Edwards wasn't the sort of man I like."

"That's a strange thing to say about a married man," Basil said.

"Well, Mr. Edwards seemed to forget he was married sometimes."

"Where were you tonight at ten past six?"

Miss Bertram jutted her chin out defiantly at the question's inference. "In the ladies."

Basil jotted something in his notebook. "Who else was in the ladies at that time?"

"I don't recall." A flattering crimson spread across Miss Bertram's pale cheek. "I was rather . . . indisposed."

"What were you and Mr. Edwards arguing about earlier?" Ginger asked.

Miss Bertram sat up defensively. "What do you mean?"

"I saw you arguing with Mr. Edwards outside. You came into the kitchen later with tears in your eyes."

"I told you, that was from the onions."

"Mrs. Davies and Miss Hanson were baking," Ginger said. "There were no onions out."

Miss Bertram pursed her lips obstinately.

"Please answer Lady Gold's question," Basil said. "Unless you'd like to discuss this down at the station."

"Fine. Mr. Edwards wanted me to meet him. He's been hounding me, saying inappropriate things, suggesting we—" Miss Bertram removed the glove on her left hand and flashed a ring. "I'm engaged. That didn't deter Mr. Edwards," she said, her eyes flashing with loathing. "In fact, he threatened to lie to George and ruin my reputation!"

Miss Bertram blinked as she worked to gain control of her emotions.

"You do realise, Miss Bertram," Basil stated, "that you have just provided motive."

Marjorie Bertram's slender jaw dropped open and a tiny "Oh" escaped. Her wide eyes darted from Basil to Ginger.

"I didn't kill him. I despised him and I'm not sorry he's dead, but it wasn't me."

"Righto," Basil said. "May I take down your address, in case I need to speak to you again?"

Basil made a note of Miss Bertram's recitation and then excused her.

Ginger, who'd taken possession of Mrs. Edwards' seat, shifted the mid-calf-length skirt of her lemon-coloured Moroccan cotton frock. It was trimmed with delightful white embroidery, which matched the trim on her sail-boat collar and dropped waist. She crossed her legs, lightly brushing the corner of Oliver's desk with her white pumps.

Miss Anna Howard tapped on the door before entering. In appearance, she was the opposite of Miss Bertram —short, blonde, and voluptuous. Where Miss Bertram showed little regret over the death of Theo Edwards, Miss Howard's round eyes were red and glassy with tears. She settled into the empty chair and dabbed her small upturned nose with a white handkerchief.

Basil only cleared his throat but Miss Howard burst into tears before he could ask his first question.

"There, there," Ginger said, patting Anna Howard on the back.

"You must excuse me. This is all such a shock. It's inconceivable, really. I simply can't believe this has happened."

"How well did you know the deceased?" Basil said.

Miss Howard lifted her quivering chin. "I loved Theo."

Ginger raised a brow at Miss Howard's use of Mr. Edwards' Christian name.

"In what capacity?" she asked gently.

"In *that* capacity. He was going to find a way to leave his wife. Such an awful woman, she is." Fresh tears erupted and ran down Miss Howard's flushed cheeks. "I wouldn't have killed him. I would've done anything for him!"

Ginger considered herself a thoroughly modern woman, but Miss Howard's unbridled confession of adultery startled her. Basil sighed like there was nothing new under the sun that he hadn't already seen.

"Where were you at ten minutes past six or shortly afterwards, Miss Howard?" Basil asked.

Miss Howard patted her face and then stared back at Basil.

"I was in the ladies."

"Popular place. Did anyone see you?"

"Um, I'm not sure."

"Did *you* see anyone?" Basil repeated in case Miss Howard did not get the full significance of the question.

"I-I don't think so. I don't remember. I'm so sorry, but this is too difficult for me. Please, may I go home now?"

Basil nodded slowly. "Just give me your address first. I'm certain I'll need to speak to you again."

Ginger had been keeping her own notes on the small notepad she carried in her burgundy silk handbag with its silver chain strap, and added Miss Howard's address to her growing list.

When Miss Howard left the office, Ginger said, "Perhaps Theo Edwards broke the news that he wasn't going to leave his wife? It's quite believable that someone with Miss Howard's temperament could act rashly."

"It's a good theory," Basil admitted. "Miss Bertram confirmed that Mr. Edwards had a perverse appetite and probably had no intention of committing solely to Miss Howard. His lack of marital loyalty gives Mrs. Edwards motive as well."

Ginger conceded. "It would be humiliating, especially if other people were starting to learn of her husband's affairs."

Basil tapped his pencil on the desk. "The *ladies* seemed to be a bustling place. Very odd that no one can vouch for another."

"Yes," Ginger said.

"Would you consider a simple cup of tea an outing?"

Ginger startled at the stark change of subject.

"Just two friends reconnecting," Basil said. "I'd like to explain—"

"You've nothing to explain, Basil. You made yourself perfectly clear when you left." And Ginger wasn't sure she could file Basil into a friendship category. Her heart couldn't manage it. He had to be either in or out, and she was prepared to put William in. Therefore, Basil was *out*.

There was a tap on the door, and Ginger released a short breath of relief at not having had to answer Basil's query.

"Mr. Piper, come on in," Basil said.

Cecil Piper took the empty chair, pushed up on his spectacles and fiddled with the bowler hat on his lap.

"He wasn't a good Christian man, you know," he stated without being asked. "I've expressed my concerns to the vicar before, but Reverend Hill only went on about grace and the like. Mr. Edwards was mean to his missus."

"Are you saying Mr. Edwards struck his wife?" Basil asked.

"There's more than one way to abuse a person, Chief Inspector."

Ginger got the impression that Mr. Piper might have been on the receiving end of such abuse in his lifetime. Perhaps from the choir director himself.

"How well do you know the Edwards family?" Basil asked.

Mr. Piper stared at his fingers as he spun the brim of his hat—stalling–as if he needed time to work out an appropriate answer.

"Not well," he finally said. "Just from church activities and the like."

"And this gave you the opportunity to form an opinion on Mr. Edwards' relationship with his wife."

"I'm not the only one, surely. You only had to have eyes and ears to witness it."

"Where were you at approximately ten minutes past six, when Mr. Edwards fell to his death?"

"I was heading to the kitchen in search of tea."

"Did anyone see you?"

"Well, I guess not. I turned back to the nave when I heard screaming."

Once again Ginger recalled the exchange of odd, possibly intimate looks she'd witnessed between Mr.

Piper and Miss Edwards. She asked, "How well do you know Miss Edwards?"

Mr. Piper jerked at the question. "N-not at all. Only from the choir, so about as well as anyone."

Ginger looked at Basil who was frowning. Mr. Piper wasn't a good liar. The question was, why was he lying?

Mrs. Davies and Reverend Markham were the next to be interviewed and provided alibis for each other as Reverend Markham had moved from Oliver's office to the kitchen for tea. They also gave Matilda Hanson an alibi, confirming her presence with them for the whole time. No, they hadn't seen Mr. Piper or any of the other suspects until they entered the church to see what all the fuss was about.

Basil instructed Mrs. Davies before she left her interview. "Please send in Mary Blythe."

Oliver arrived with Mary and protested. "Surely this isn't necessary. Mary's been through a trauma, and now our wedding must be postponed. It's all very trying."

"We'll make it as brief as possible," Basil said.

Poor Mary Blythe did look a sight. Her brunette hair had fallen out of its pins, and the front panel of her green cotton frock was excessively wrinkled. She crumpled into a ball in the chair, and Ginger fought the urge to encourage her to sit up straight.

"I'm so sorry this has happened so close to what was meant to be your happy day," Ginger said.

Mary wept into her handkerchief. "It's awful, simply awful. I don't know what I'm going to do."

"Now, now. You'll still get married. Next weekend or

the week after. It won't make much difference in the long run."

Mary glanced up at Ginger with teary eyes. "I hope you're right."

"Miss Blythe," Basil said, looking rather uncomfortable. "You entered the church shortly after Mr. Edwards fell. Where were you coming from?"

"Home. I've been ill, nerves I think."

"So you entered from the main entrance of the church?"

"Yes."

"Did you see anyone enter or exit the rear balcony stairwell?"

Mary shook her head. "No."

"Did you go up to the balcony at all today?"

Mary's red eyes grew rounder. "No. I only just arrived. I was late for my meeting with Oliver and Reverend Markham."

Ginger shot Basil a look, which begged for compassion. Basil sighed. "Very well, Miss Blythe," Basil said. "That shall be all for now."

Oliver had been waiting in the passageway and immediately put a protective arm around Mary as she left.

"You can speak to her again tomorrow if you must," Ginger said, "but I do believe the girl is ready to collapse from exhaustion. Did you see the circles under her eyes? She must not be sleeping well."

"Indeed."

"Mr. Piper was exceptionally vague," Ginger continued, aware that she was rambling. She didn't want to give

Basil the opportunity to revisit his question about meeting for a friendly cup of tea. "I think there's more to the story about why he disliked Mr. Edwards. And he was definitely lying about his connection to Miss Edwards."

"Ginger?"

Ginger forced herself to look Basil in the eye.

"Yes?"

"Take a breath. I won't repeat my invitation." He grinned. "Today."

Ginger's throat had grown dry, and she was in sudden need of a glass of water, cup of tea, or quite possibly, something stronger.

Basil closed his notepad and returned it to his suit pocket. "We need to find the murder weapon."

"Yes," Ginger said, happy to keep their conversation on the case. "It has to be in this building somewhere."

"I'll see what my constables have come up with."

Ginger gathered her handbag, but before she could get to her feet, Basil asked her to remain for another minute.

"Yes, what is it?" she said.

"I need to apologise."

"No, you don't."

"I want to."

"She was your wife."

"But I was in love with you."

*Was?* Ginger inhaled, suddenly finding it hard to breathe.

"I'm still in love with you."

She glared at him boldly. "Then why did you stay away for so long?"

"It's a long journey to South Africa. I was a fool to go so far away, but at the time I wasn't in my right mind."

"And you're in your right mind now?"

"Yes."

Ginger wanted to believe him, but she was unsure if she could trust again. As much as she tried to pretend it was otherwise, as much as she convinced herself that she had no right to feel offended by a man grieving his estranged wife, Basil's departure had hurt her deeply.

The office door, left ajar, was suddenly flung open and William Beale filled the space.

Ginger gawked. "William!"

"Darling. Hill convinced the police to let me in. I needed to be sure that you were all right."

"I'm fine," Ginger said, holding in her aggravation. "I told you that on the telephone."

"But a man's been murdered. You could be in danger."

Basil stood and strode to William's side. He stretched out a hand. "I'm Chief Inspector Basil Reed. I can assure you that Lady Gold is safe with me."

William stiffened. "I am quite aware of who you are, Chief Inspector." His unspoken words resounded loudly. *Lady Gold is indeed not safe alone with you.* "I'm Captain William Beale." He turned to Ginger and extended his arm. "Shall we go?"

Ginger burned with indignation. She nearly refused him, but she didn't dare make a scene.

"Of course." Smiling at Basil, she added, "If you need my assistance, you know where to find me."

# CHAPTER NINE

Felicia had invited Matilda Hanson to luncheon the next day. Miss Hanson, an intelligent and pretty girl, resembled the Hollywood icon Clara Bow with her teardrop face and rosebud lips. While going through a personal crisis, she and Felicia had formed a friendship. She had been a long-term guest at Hartigan House, though her presence had proved to be a social hardship for Ambrosia who struggled with the mixing of the classes. The matron sat stiffly at the head of the dining room table, looking put out.

"Hello, Matilda," Ginger said giving Matilda a welcoming embrace before taking her seat at the table. "Good afternoon, everyone."

"You're rather chipper today," Louisa remarked. "I couldn't sleep a wink last night after yesterday's horrific events. Poor Mary Blythe. Imagine having your wedding disrupted like that. Now, what are they going to do?"

"The ceremony has been postponed," Ginger said, with

a quick glance at Matilda. Their guest's gaze had averted to her lap but her expression revealed no dismay. "July weddings are as lovely as those in June."

"Poor Mary," Louisa repeated.

Ginger simply nodded. She wondered at Oliver's words, "The Lord moves in mysterious ways." Perhaps this was a way out for Oliver. Mary was a sweet girl, but Ginger's feeling that she was the wrong match for the vicar had only intensified.

Lizzie and Grace produced Mrs. Beasley's delectable offering of pea soup, followed by grilled mackerel and parsnips in cream sauce. Boss sat at Ginger's feet in energetic anticipation, and she sneaked him a piece of fish.

"It really is the stuff of novels," Felicia said. "Perhaps I should write a book now that I live in London."

"Have you written anything so far?" Haley asked.

"Well, no," Felicia admitted. "But I could start. I simply do need a hobby, or I'm bound to go back to reckless partying."

"Oh, please," Ginger said with a smile. "*Do* write a book."

"I can't imagine writing a book," Louisa said. She paused before drinking the final spoonful of soup. "I think it would be quite a lot of work."

"One needs a tremendous imagination," Ambrosia added. "I do think Felicia has more than enough of that. Child, if you must insist on attempting such a common occupation, I do hope you don't write mysteries. Very lowbrow. One with good breeding should compose literary works in the vein of Sir Walter Scott or Rudyard Kipling."

Ginger suspected Ambrosia's author choices had to do with the title in the first case (Sir) and the well-known place of birth of the other (the Bombay Presidency of British India) and not because she'd actually read the writers.

"I wish I could pen poems," Felicia gushed. "Poets are so mysterious and awe-inspiring, and poems wouldn't take nearly so long to write. Louisa lent me her copy of Robert Frost's latest collection. He recently won a Pulitzer Prize. Can you imagine? I don't think I could draft a poem to save my life."

Haley shook her head, her dark curls springing loose. "Me, neither. I don't have a creative bone in my body."

"I'm not a big fan of his poem *Nothing Gold Can Stay*," Felicia admitted. "Not for literary reasons, of course. Just a superstitious issue over the word, 'gold.'"

Ginger knew the octave well, being in possession of her own copy of the American poet's work, and began reciting.

Nature's first green is gold,

her hardest hue to hold.

Her early leaf's a flower;

but only so an hour.

Then leaf subsides to leaf.

So Eden sank to grief,

So dawn goes down to day.

Nothing gold can stay.

Ambrosia's silver fork landed on her china dish with a clang. "What does that even mean? *Leaf subsides to leaf.* It's just a bunch of nonsense."

"It's an allegory, Grandmama," Felicia said. "It's not meant to be taken literally."

"If one has something to say," Ambrosia said, "one should say it plainly. Is the man even English?"

"He's American," Ginger said. She had to bite her lip to keep from smiling.

"Ah," Ambrosia said as if that explained things.

"Although, he did live in London for a few years before the war," Ginger added.

"Foreigners," Ambrosia huffed. "Can't be trusted."

"The poem is a *felix culpa*," Matilda said. "It's Latin for lucky unluckiness."

Ambrosia rested her teacup and set a rare gaze on her guest. "What on earth are you talking about, Miss Hanson?"

Matilda withered slightly under the dowager's glare, and Ginger felt she should jump in to save her.

"*Felix culpe* is a term used when there are fortunate consequences to an unfortunate event. The Catholics use the term for 'blessed fall,' as in the fall of man leading to the redemption of humankind through the resurrection."

Searching for a new fault, Ambrosia narrowed her grey eyes on Matilda Hanson. "Are you a Catholic?"

"I'm not, madam," Matilda replied. "Church of England, through and through."

"Felicia," Louisa whined, "I beg you not to start writing

a book while I'm a guest. I'll simply be bored to tears without you to entertain me."

"How long shall we, ahem, have the pleasure of your company?" Ambrosia asked.

Ginger was quite sure her intended meaning was, *How long until you leave?*

"I don't know," Louisa responded. "Mama is quite adamant I come home immediately, but I can't stand the notion of living under her roof. She's so suffocating! I get a letter from her every day." Louisa rang for her maid. "Jenny!" she said as the girl entered. "Get me my fan. The heat is exhausting me."

Jenny frowned and scampered away to do as she was told. Louisa, noticing the mild stares of disapproval, huffed. "It's so hard to find a good maid."

Ambrosia stared at Ginger with a stern look of disapproval. Louisa was indeed a force to be reckoned with. No one was more aware of that than Ginger. At least Louisa would be kept out of Ambrosia's hair with her commitment to work at the shop.

Ginger smiled at her stepsister. "Shall we go?"

"Go?" Louisa said with a pout.

"To Feathers & Flair!" Ginger said dramatically. "Today's your first day as my new employee."

# CHAPTER TEN

*A*fter dropping Louisa off at Feathers & Flair and calming Madame Roux with hopeful reassurances that Louisa would make a fine addition to the staff, Ginger headed to St. George's Church. She was concerned about Oliver's emotional wellbeing, which was why Boss sat in the passenger seat, panting happily with his nose pressed against the window. There was nothing like a little unconditional love from a gentle animal to calm the soul. Ginger was just happy that Clement had got the tyre fixed so quickly. A patch and a bit of air didn't take a lot of time.

An unwelcoming rope blocked off the front entrance —a disturbing and ominous sign, Ginger thought. A scar of violence on what was meant to be a place of peace and sanctity.

"This way, Bossy," Ginger said as she headed down the stone pathway along the side of the church. She knocked on the hall door then pulled the cord that rang a small iron bell.

The wooden door swung open. Ginger was surprised to find Matilda Hanson standing there in her blue day dress and simple pumps, with her short brunette hair pinned off her face.

"Oh, hello again, Matilda." Ginger chided herself for not asking her lunch guest about her plans for the rest of the day.

"Lady Gold, come in." With Boss at her heels, Ginger followed her friend into the kitchen. "Thanks again for the lovely luncheon."

"I'm sure it's Felicia who deserves the thanks, but you are always welcome. You are family now."

Matilda smiled with gratitude, and it warmed Ginger's heart. Matilda had lost a child and almost her life, and Ginger was delighted to see how well she was doing. Of course, the fact that there had been a child at all had to be kept a secret at all costs, and in that regard, Matilda grieved her loss alone. At least her reputation had been saved.

"I'm helping Mrs. Davies reorganise now that the wedding is postponed," Matilda offered when they entered the kitchen.

"Have they set a new date?" Ginger asked.

"Not that I'm aware of," Matilda said, keeping her gaze averted. "You can ask Reverend Hill yourself. We were just about to break for tea."

As if conjured up, Oliver entered just as Matilda

finished speaking. He heartily welcomed Ginger. "So nice to see you again so soon, even though the circumstances are less than pleasant." He squatted to scrub Boss behind his pointy ears. "Hello there, fellow." In a gesture Ginger had never seen before, Oliver swooped the small dog into his arms and let the pup lick his face. Ginger had been right to bring him along.

"Such a good dog, you are," Oliver said, smiling genuinely.

"Miss Hanson kindly invited me to join you for tea," Ginger said.

"Of course!" Oliver turned to Mrs. Davies and opened his mouth, but Mrs. Davies was already setting a fourth place at the plain, but functional, kitchen table.

Matilda poured the tea, fumbling slightly with Oliver's cup. "So sorry," she said.

Oliver, who'd been watching her intently, waved away her apology. "Not to worry."

Ginger couldn't help noticing how the two of them watched each other. They clearly shared a genuine affection for one another.

Mrs. Davies set out anchovy canapés and eggs with *foie gras*. "These will have to be thrown out soon."

Ginger took in the vast amount of *hors d'oeuvres* meant for Oliver and Mary's reception, and her stomach knotted. "I'm afraid I've just eaten a rather large luncheon, Mrs. Davies. I hope you don't mind if I just drink tea.

"Please have something, Lady Gold. We must all do what we can."

Ginger and Matilda each took one egg half and a slice of cheese to appease the hard-working church secretary.

"Delicious," Ginger said, meaning it.

Despite the look of it, Mrs. Davies was an expert cook.

"Your hard work is not in vain, Mrs. Davies," Oliver said keeping positive. "We'll use the food intended for the reception at the next Child Wellness Project hot meal tomorrow night." He let out a short breath. "A silver lining for the street children."

Ginger laid a hand on Oliver's arm. "I'm so sorry this has happened, Oliver."

"Not the best way to begin one's lives together," he said.

"A month won't kill either of you," Mrs. Davies said.

"Mary seems to think it will."

There was an uncomfortable silence where everyone took the opportunity to sip their tea and nibble a *canapé*. Ginger noted tension between Oliver and Matilda, but maybe she was just imagining things. Sometimes her romantic tendencies, for *other* people, got in the way of practicality.

"Reverend Markham's going to take the service on Sunday," Oliver said with a sigh. "The police have promised the rope will be removed tomorrow afternoon."

"That'll be nice," Mrs. Davies said.

Ginger looked at Matilda. Before Miss Hanson had come to Ginger's attention three months earlier, she had been a student at the London Medical School for Women.

"Have you registered for the autumn term, Miss Hanson?" Ginger asked.

Matilda set her teacup on its saucer. "Actually, no."

Ginger's jaw grew slack in astonishment. "Really? Why not?"

"I've decided not to go back to medical school."

"I'm sure I don't understand why," Ginger said. "You did so well there. It's your dream to become a doctor."

"It *was* my dream," Matilda said softly. "My focus has changed since—I've decided to become a midwife."

Ginger blinked. "A midwife?"

"I want to help women to safely and successfully bring children into the world," Matilda explained. "Medicine is very demanding, as I'm sure you know—being a friend of Miss Higgins. I want to have more time for people than books."

Ginger had to concede that she saw very little of Haley, and that Haley was always strapped for time to engage in anything not study or medicine related.

"I'm sure you'll make a fine midwife," Ginger said with all sincerity.

Oliver's eyes shone with kindness and affection. "Miss Hanson's been a big help to Mrs. Davies and me, too,"

Matilda blushed. "I'm happy to do it. It gives me a real sense of satisfaction to serve the church. For the first time, I feel at peace, and I'm grateful to God for it."

"Well, in that case," Ginger said, "I'm very happy for you." Ginger pushed away from the table and addressed Oliver. "Do you mind if I take another look in the church?"

"Not at all," Oliver said.

"Perhaps you'd like to join me?"

Oliver didn't appear overly eager at the suggestion, but he stood to accompany Ginger nonetheless.

Matilda began to clear the table, and she and Mrs. Davies returned to their tasks in the kitchen.

Once Ginger had Oliver in the passage, she lowered her voice and asked pointedly, "Are you sure the wedding shouldn't be *postponed?*"

"Well, since we were meant to be wed the day after tomorrow—"

"You know what I mean, Oliver Hill." Ginger called for Boss, who was licking his lips after eating the anchovy Ginger had slipped him, to keep up as they strolled to Oliver's office. "I'm suggesting indefinitely. I know this is very forward of me, and I'm trying to be delicate—"

"I appreciate your candour, Ginger." Oliver drew a hand over his oiled hair, capturing stray ginger curls. "I know I've made a huge mistake."

Ginger patted his arm. "It's not too late to change things."

"But it is. I've asked, and she's accepted. We've made a public announcement. We're betrothed. I would be seen as a scoundrel and a louse. The diocese would remove me from St. George's and probably assign me to some country church where I'd have to start again from scratch. I do care for my parishioners here. Oh dear Lord, what have I got myself into?"

"Oliver, perhaps you should sit down."

"Yes, right." Oliver pulled the chair behind his desk

and sat. "If I marry Mary, I'll be miserable, and if I don't marry her, I'll be miserable. See, I'm too selfish to be a vicar. I'm only thinking about myself. I should consider another vocation."

"Do you have any whisky stashed away in here somewhere?" Ginger asked.

"Oh, yes, I do, actually. It's not too early?"

Ginger shook her head. "Sometimes circumstances call for an early start."

"Good thinking." Oliver pulled out two glasses and a bottle of whisky, three-quarters full, from his desk drawer.

"None for me," Ginger said. "But, please, go ahead."

Oliver poured for himself and took a long pull. He inhaled deeply. "Thank you, Ginger. I just need a moment to gain perspective."

"Exactly. Now, let's think about this. What if Mary has changed her mind?"

"Then, I suppose I'd be released from any obligation I have to her, but believe me, she has her heart set on marriage. She's quite upset about this disruption."

"Perhaps she's only saying what she thinks you want to hear."

Oliver lowered his chin. "Do you think so?"

"Women can be quite convincing when they want to be. Would it be all right with you if I had a chat with her? Perhaps speaking to another lady would calm her and help her to sort out her emotions. She might be feeling the same way you are, and also thinking there's no way out."

"Oh, that would be fabulous. Not that I want any shame or humiliation to befall Mary. I do care for her."

"Leave it to me." Ginger stood and brushed the wrinkles from her silk brown-and-turquoise crêpe dress and matching spring jacket. "Now, I really do want to take another look at the crime scene."

# CHAPTER ELEVEN

*W*as it really only yesterday that Ginger had been rehearsing with the choir, Mr. Theo Edwards alive and well, and Oliver pacing in anticipation of the vows he was yet to make?

Ginger looked up to the rail where Mr. Edwards had toppled over. Not an actual rail, but a short stone wall. St. George's Church was over three hundred years old. People had been shorter back then, Ginger mused. Mr. Edwards was only average in height, yet a good push could easily see him lose his balance and topple over, especially with a conk on the head beforehand.

The instrument used to inflict that wound hadn't been found even though Scotland Yard had had their best constables searching.

The cleaning ladies would soon arrive to wash away the blood, and soon all evidence of Mr. Edwards' demise would be erased. There would be a funeral at St. George's before there would be a wedding. Ginger wondered if Basil planned to return with the constable who would remove the rope and make public access official. Her heart skipped at the thought of seeing him again, but she quickly chastised herself. Basil Reed was in her *past*.

Ginger pulled on the door to the stone stairwell that led to the balcony and noticed how it didn't make a sound. Such an observation the day before would've been nearly impossible with all the noise and carrying on of the witnesses echoing through the sanctuary. Further examination confirmed to Ginger that the hinges had been recently oiled. The work of Mr. Simpson, the sexton, or a murderer's premeditation?

Upstairs, Ginger examined the area where Mr. Edwards had fallen. A streak of blood stained the stonework. Had Mr. Edwards touched the wound on his head before trying to prevent his fall?

Boss sniffed the area.

"What do you smell, Bossy? The murderer?"

How long exactly would it take someone to make it back to the nave? Everyone who hadn't been there when the fall occurred had entered within seconds. Whoever pushed Mr. Edwards had raced down and put on a good show.

Ginger checked her wristwatch then ran from the area where Mr. Edwards had been hit and pushed, along the balcony, to the second exit, and down the staircase that opened up by the main entrance. Boss chased her, thinking it was great fun.

She rechecked her watch. Eighteen seconds.

More than enough time for one to join the crowd after the fact without one's whereabouts being questioned.

Boss stood with his front paws on the steps, panting, eyes eager to play the game again.

Ginger chuckled and took the steps back up to the balcony in search of any clue that might jump out at her from this vantage point, but she saw nothing—only Boss sitting proudly at the top as he rejoiced in his win.

Sitting on the organ bench, Ginger imagined Mrs. Esme Edwards playing. From this position, the organist could see the parishioners, the vicar's pulpit, and the choir director's podium, but not the choir members. When Ginger had witnessed Mr. Edwards looking upwards, it was his wife he'd been glaring at.

Ginger placed her hands on the keys. She couldn't resist the temptation and began to play. Surely, Oliver wouldn't mind. She was thankful now that her father had insisted on all those lessons she'd had as a child. Her fingers tickled the keys expertly, and a sweet melody lifted to the heavens, ringing bright and lovely until she hit the last note.

"Oh, mercy, Boss. What was that?"

Ginger hit the key again and grimaced. Instead of a clear, sustained note, it sounded more like the smelly raspberry that Boss was often guilty of producing. He barked as if to say, "that wasn't me," and started sniffing at the wall where it met up with the organ. He yipped again.

"What is it, Boss?"

The organ was on wheels, and when Ginger tugged at

the frame, it slid away from the stone alcove, revealing unexposed pipes.

"Aha," she said, having discovered the problem. The pipe was inserted backwards. She grinned at Boss. "Oliver needs to give the organ tuner a good talking to."

Easily, she slipped the pipe out of its hold and immediately wished she was wearing gloves. There, near the bottom where the pipe tapered to a small opening, was blood.

"Well, Boss," she said. "I think we've found the murder weapon."

OLIVER MADE the call to Scotland Yard, and half an hour later Basil arrived along with Sergeant Scott and a constable.

When Ginger came into view, Basil smiled. "It's a pleasure as always," he said, his hazel eyes glinting with playfulness. "Of course, I wasn't at all surprised when Reverend Hill said you were here. Nor was I surprised when he said you'd made the discovery."

Ginger wasn't sure how to process this new, happy-go-lucky Basil Reed who encased his compliments with blatant flirting.

She stood tall with her hands clasped in front. "I only wished to play the organ, Chief Inspector. The bad note was the giveaway. The next person to play was bound to discover it. I assure you, I did nothing special."

"Yet, it was you who played the organ and found the

clue, Lady Gold. Providence is on your side, once again. Now, will you kindly show us what you discovered?"

Ginger huffed. She didn't like the emotions swirling in her heart, not one bit. Basil Reed had a way of getting under her skin, but she must be resolute. She *had* moved on.

"This way," she said then opened the door to the balcony. She waved for Basil and his men to go ahead, but Basil shook his head.

"Please, ladies first."

Ginger huffed again, knowing that Basil had a good view of her backside. She no longer cared what Basil Reed thought of her.

She *didn't*.

"This is how I found it," she explained, then pressed the corresponding key which released a sound like a cat with its tail in the door. "I pulled the organ away from the wall to try to identify the cause of the sour note and found the bent pipe. It had been inserted incorrectly."

Wearing gloves, Basil squatted and slipped the pipe out of its position.

"And there's blood," Ginger added, quite unnecessarily, as the dried brown spots were evident to the naked eye.

"Nicely done," Basil said, standing. "I'll get the Yard to examine it for prints."

"You'll have to contact the tuner for elimination prints," Ginger said.

Basil looked at her. "Of course."

"And test the blood type," Ginger said. "Haley's been

studying blood grouping. Did you know they've categorised human blood into four types?"

Basil grinned easily. "Yes, our laboratories are fully aware of the latest forensic developments, Ginger."

Ginger turned away feeling sheepish at her attempt to appear better informed than Basil. What was the matter with her? Basil was a good detective. He knew how to do his job.

Sergeant Scott and the constable did another cursory search of the organ and balcony area before leaving. Basil returned to the spot where Mr. Edwards had fallen.

"Edwards came up the steps of the vestry, we assume to speak to his wife," he said, walking down the balcony towards the back of the church where the organ was located. "They argued, and as he left, she searched for a weapon. Knowing organs, she'd know the mechanics of how one works, that the pipes aren't very heavy, and easily removed. In her rage, Esme Edwards pulled the organ out, removed the closest pipe, ran after her husband, hit him across the head, and pushed him over the rail.

"Then, realising what she'd done, quickly put the pipe back and pushed the organ to the wall, ran down the rear stairwell and entered the nave from the hall side of the church with some of the others."

"It's a good theory," Ginger said. "But I have a hard time believing a lady would kill her husband over a disagreement on how the organ was being played."

"Women have killed their husbands over less."

"Undoubtedly."

"Would you like to have dinner with me tonight?"

Ginger wasn't often caught unawares, but Basil had a way of making her feel off-kilter, especially with this sudden change of subject. "I . . . I can't. I'm having dinner with William."

"But you would've otherwise?"

"I didn't say that. No. I'm sure William would highly disapprove."

"Forgive me, but I'm not interested in gaining Captain Beale's approval."

"Well, then, I disapprove."

Basil grinned. "I don't believe you do."

"I said I do, so I do."

"You're lying to yourself." He stepped closer. The scent of Basil Reed, which Ginger had missed so much, assaulted her senses.

"I'm not." Her words came out as a pathetic whimper.

"You are. You'd rather have dinner with me."

Ginger sidestepped Basil and put as much distance between them as the narrow balcony would allow.

"Chief Inspector Reed! You are boorish. Let's keep things professional, shall we?" She walked with determined strides and headed back down to the nave, her neck bristling at the sound of Basil chuckling behind her.

# CHAPTER TWELVE

The Edwards family lived in a modest, middle-class red-brick house in a cul-de-sac with other identical houses. Ginger had agreed to meet Basil there the next morning. Basil, of course, could question the two women on his own, but it gratified Ginger to know that he found some interviews uncomfortable and that her presence as a female really did help put interviewees at ease.

Basil was already there, leaning against his forest-green Austin 7 with his arms crossed and the brim of his trilby pulled low to ward off the glare of the morning sun.

She pulled up behind him and set her handbrake.

"You stay here, Boss," she said then patted him on his black-and-white head to ease the pup's disappointment. "I won't be long."

Basil was at her door and opened it for her before she had a chance to get out.

"Thank you," she said politely. "And good morning."

"Good morning to you, Lady Gold." His hazel eyes glinted with humour, infuriating Ginger. What on earth did he find so funny at this time of the day?

"Did you have a pleasant evening?" Basil asked.

The question sounded innocuous, a simple attempt at making polite conversation, but Ginger knew that Basil was aware that she'd had dinner with William, and she wasn't about to tell Basil about any of that. Besides, the evening had proven rather dull next to everything else that had been happening.

"It was fine," she replied. "Yours?"

"Uneventful."

A black mourning ribbon had been attached to the door, alerting the neighbours to a death in the family. Mrs. Edwards responded to Basil's knock.

The house was clean and tidy, the walls painted a bright white, with burgundy tiled floors and matching burgundy, printed drapery. The furniture was stained a dark brown and complemented the plush, powder-blue fabric of the two armchairs and sofa.

"We don't have a maid," Mrs. Edwards said, "so I'll have to get the tea myself."

"This isn't a social call, so tea won't be required," Basil said. "Please ask Miss Edwards to join us. We'll try to be as quick as we can."

"Very well," Mrs. Edwards muttered. She shuffled out of the room with drooping shoulders, and Ginger felt a stab of pity. Mrs. Edwards may not have loved her husband, but his death was certain to change her life, and quite possibly not for the better.

Unlike Mrs. Edwards, Miss Edwards was clothed in black—a shiny rayon frock, loose-fitting with a waistband low on her hips and a skirt that narrowed slightly just above her ankles. Her matted, blue bedroom slippers were jarring in contrast.

"Hello, again," she said timidly as she took one of the armchairs. Ginger and Basil were seated on the sofa, leaving the second chair for Mrs. Edwards.

An uncomfortable silence descended, and Ginger felt the need to bridge it.

"Mrs. Edwards, Miss Edwards, I just want to extend my condolences, once again. We wouldn't dream of intruding at such a time as this if it weren't to find out who took Mr. Edwards' life."

Basil shot her a look, but Ginger felt validated when Mrs. Edwards relaxed in her chair and said, "Of course. We'll cooperate in any way we can."

"Mrs. Edwards," Basil started, "I hate to bring this up, but I must ask, how was your relationship with your husband."

Esme Edwards stilled.

"What goes on between a husband and wife is a private affair, Chief Inspector. Surely, you of all people should know that."

Ginger grimaced. Mrs. Edwards certainly had a sharp tongue on her. But she had a point. Anyone who read the papers would know about Basil Reed's troubled marriage with his deceased wife. The situation surrounding Emelia's death was indeed scandalous.

"This interview isn't about me, Mrs. Edwards."

Mrs. Edwards huffed. "Our marriage wasn't ideal. From the beginning, I knew I'd made a mistake—"

Miss Edwards emitted a soft, disapproving mewing sound. Mrs. Edwards glared at her, then continued.

"But, I'd made my bed, and I had to lie on it."

"You realise that gives you motive," Basil said.

Mrs. Edwards blinked in confusion. "Motive? For what?"

"For killing your husband," Ginger said gently.

Mrs. Edwards bristled like an old cockerel. "I did no such thing. I could name a dozen or more married ladies who'd say the same thing, that their marriage was a mistake, but they're not all about to go and do away with their husbands. Like I said, I made my bed and I was willing to lie on it until I died."

"Even so," Basil said. "We shall be checking your financial records to see just how you benefit from your husband's death."

"How on earth would I benefit from that? Theo was the breadwinner. What are Catherine and I going to do now? We'll both have to get jobs. Whatever you're thinking, Theo's death is not good for either of us."

"Did your husband have a life insurance policy?"

"A *what*?"

"It's a rather new provision," Ginger said. "One can purchase insurance for one's life. Much like one does for an automobile, should there be an accident."

"Are you comparing my husband to a motorcar?"

"No. Just the insurance part is comparable. For instance, Mr. Edwards may have bought insurance on his life, so that when he died, you and Catherine would be provided for financially."

Mrs. Edwards perked up. "Really?" Then her shoulders deflated. "No. Theo only thought of himself. In his mind, he was invincible." Her hand went to her throat. "I'm sure that man left us nothing but bills to pay."

"Where were you last night at ten minutes past six?" Basil asked

"Theo had paused the rehearsal. I went downstairs to visit the ladies."

Basil frowned. "The *ladies* seems to be a popular destination."

"It's quite natural, I assure you," Mrs. Edwards said. "Especially if one had had a cup of tea beforehand."

"Did you use the stairs that lead to the vestry?" Ginger asked. She hadn't seen Mrs. Edwards come down that way.

"No. The ones that come out by the entrance. They're closer to the organ loft."

"Did you speak to your husband beforehand?" Basil asked.

"Actually, I didn't. He was ranting as usual, going on about how he was going to remove me from my position as chief organist, but I just ignored him. He's been threatening to dispose of me for years."

"That must've made you angry?" Basil said. "Life shall be easier now without him around to constantly berate you."

Esme Edwards narrowed her eyes and glared. "Like I said before, Chief Inspector, he supported me and

Catherine. It shall not be easier. I didn't kill my husband."

"Miss Edwards," Basil said, turning his gaze to the grieving sister. "I'm sorry for your loss. Can you bear to answer a couple of questions?"

Catherine Edwards sniffed. "Anything to help catch the person who did this."

"Where were you when your brother fell?"

"I was in the ladies."

"Did anyone see you?"

"I don't think so."

Basil glanced at Ginger, his eyes flashing disbelief. How many women did this ladies' room accommodate, and how was it possible for none to see the others?

"Did you hear anyone else in the lavatory?" Ginger asked. "Voices?"

"I-I don't recall."

"Very well," Basil said as he got to his feet. "That shall be all for now, but please don't leave London without letting me know."

Outside, as they walked back to their motorcars, Ginger said, "You were rather hard on poor Mrs. Edwards."

"Spouses are often the perpetrators in domestic crimes."

Ginger gaped. "This coming from *you*?" Basil had had the unfortunate experience of being a prime suspect in a similar situation.

"I said often, not always." Basil reached for Ginger's

motorcar door and pulled it open. "So, tell me about Captain William Beale."

Ginger huffed as she slid inside, pushing Boss back to his seat on the passenger side. "I shall not."

Basil's hazel eyes bore down on her. They were warm and *interested*. In *her*. He grinned crookedly in the way that made Ginger's heart flutter and her knees turn to jelly. Blast that man!

"I think it's only fair that I know whom I'm up against," he said.

Ginger started the engine. "You've got a nerve, Chief Inspector." She closed her door, a mite harder than needed, and put the gear into reverse.

eathers & Flair was Ginger's Regent Street dress shop. It was uncommon for a lady to own her own business, and Ginger felt gratified at the example she set for the next generation of young women coming up behind her.

Like her stepsister, Louisa.

Ginger set Boss down on the glossy marble floor. "To the back, young man," she instructed, then smiled as the little dog obediently crossed the marble floor to the red velvet curtains that separated the front of the shop from the back. He disappeared to where his second bed and food bowl were situated.

The white ceilings were high, with gold-painted mouldings trimming the walls and hollows from which the electric chandeliers were hung.

Madame Roux, the shop's competent and dependable manager, approached with a look of relief on her face.

"Lady Gold. Have you come to fetch Miss Hartigan?"

"She's only been here a couple of hours," Ginger said with concern. Why was her manager so eager to be relieved of Louisa's presence? "I've come to do some work," she added. She felt that it was important that she put in an appearance at least a few days a week to oversee operations. "Where is my sister?"

The bell above the door rang, and a matronly-looking lady entered.

Madame Roux whispered to Ginger. "She's in the back." Then to the customer, "Hello, Lady Cunningham! How may I be of service today?"

Lady Cunningham proceeded to inform Madame Roux of a forthcoming christening—she couldn't wear the same dress she'd worn to the last one.

Ginger smiled at the ease with which Madame Roux guided Lady Cunningham into choosing the perfect gown.

Louisa was in the back trying on dresses.

"Oh, Ginger," she said, on seeing her. "These just came in from Paris."

"Why are you trying them on? They should be recorded in our books and taken upstairs."

The second floor was where the factory dresses were displayed.

Louisa twirled in front of the mirror. "Dora is taking care of that."

"It's *Dorothy*," Ginger and Emma said together. Emma Miller was Ginger's junior seamstress. She leaned over the Singer sewing machine and madly rocked the floor pedal with her foot.

"Louisa, please put on your own clothes and then help Dorothy by taking the rest of the frocks upstairs."

Louisa huffed. "Fine. If you insist. But I refuse to call beautiful dresses *frocks*. It sounds so frumpy."

Louisa disappeared into the changing cubicle.

Ginger shrugged apologetically at Emma who'd stopped sewing at Louisa's affront. "I think she's home-sick," Ginger provided, lamely.

Over the next few hours, Ginger assisted Madame Roux with customers, oversaw Dorothy and Louisa's progress upstairs, and did a bit of bookwork at the front desk.

The telephone rang—a gorgeous cream and gold machine with a modern bar-shaped handset with the receiver at one end, the transmitter at the other, and attached to a curly cord—and Madame Roux answered. She held her palm over the mouthpiece and whispered to Ginger, "Chief Inspector Reed for you, Lady Gold."

Ginger let out a short breath. Why would the chief inspector call here? He must have more information about the Theo Edwards' case, evidently.

Ginger claimed the handset and waited for Madame Roux to move politely out of hearing range.

"Hello, Chief Inspector."

"Lady Gold. I'm sorry to ring you at your shop. Your butler, Pippins, told me I might find you there."

"It's quite all right. Do you have news?"

"I do, and I'm afraid it's not pleasant. I've just arrested Mrs. Edwards for the alleged murder of her husband."

"On what evidence?"

"It turns out that Mr. Edwards *had* purchased life insurance. It appears that he was a progressive thinker."

"That doesn't mean—"

"It was at Superintendent Morris' insistence."

Ginger snorted. She and the superintendent didn't see eye to eye on many things.

"Well, I appreciate you letting me know," Ginger said.

"Any reason to talk to you is a good one," Basil said. Ginger could hear the smile in his voice, and she pinched her lips together in annoyance.

"Would you have dinner with me tonight?"

Ginger held the handset away from her ear and stared at it. Basil Reed was persistent if nothing else.

Returning the receiver to her ear, she said stiffly, "I'm afraid I'm otherwise engaged. Good day, Chief Inspector Reed." She hung up quickly because being rude was better than being weak, and there was something deep inside urging her to say *yes*.

"You must've heard about Oliver and Mary's wedding postponement," Louisa was saying to Dorothy when Ginger checked in on the second level. "The poor bride-to-be. Can you imagine a body dropping two nights before your wedding? I mean holy mackerel!"

Ginger glanced at Dorothy who kept her gaze on the floor. Dorothy had had hopes of being a minister's wife, Oliver's specifically, but he had chosen Mary over her.

Madame Roux's voice echoed up the stairs. "Lady Gold. Another telephone call for you."

Who could it be this time? Basil again?

It was the police but not Basil, and she barely

contained her amazement. Esme Edwards was requesting that Ginger visit her at the Scotland Yard holding cell.

"Yes, of course," she responded to the constable. "I'm on my way."

"Madame Roux," Ginger said as she gathered her silk brocaded Bohemian jacket and smoothed out the fringe. "I'll leave things in your competent hands."

"And Miss Hartigan?" Madame Roux asked with a slight plea.

"She can remain until the end of the day."

Louisa appeared at the bottom of the stairs making Ginger's announcement convenient. "I'll see you back at the house, Louisa."

"You're leaving?"

"Yes. The four of you can manage quite well without me."

"But, how am I to get home?"

"You must take a taxicab. And please don't forget to bring Boss!"

# CHAPTER FOURTEEN

Ginger supposed it would've taken less time to use the tube to get from Regent Street to Scotland Yard along the Victoria Embankment. Oxford Circus station was only a five-minute walk from Feathers & Flair. Of course, a taxicab was always an option too. However, Ginger preferred her Crossley, even though she still found driving on the left somewhat taxing. She'd learned to drive in Boston and her natural instinct was to stay on the right. But Ginger wasn't the kind who backed away from a challenge.

She mused about those particular tests as she navigated around populated wooden buses, horse-drawn carriages, and pedestrians who seemed to have a death wish. Her father had forced her very first life challenge upon her when he took her away from London, and everything and everyone she'd known, to move to Boston. That trial had been doubled with the introduction of her new stepmother, to whom she'd never felt really close. Of course, Louisa's birth was a blessing, but she had a difficult temperament. Then there was Father's illness and his passing away, and the most significant life test of them all —the Great War and losing her husband, Daniel, Lord Gold.

A series of horns blasting in her direction brought her out of her reverie. Already she was at Trafalgar Square and made the difficult negotiation onto Whitehall and then into the parking area behind Scotland Yard.

Not surprisingly, Basil was there, presumably waiting for her. His Savile Row suit fitted him perfectly as he stood straight and tall, staring at her. His hair was trimmed neatly and oiled, causing the grey at his temples to shine. The lines around his warm hazel eyes deepened as he smiled.

"Hello, Chief Inspector Reed," Ginger said as she approached him. She prided herself on sounding in control of her emotions, entirely professional, and not at all *attracted*.

"Good day, Lady Gold," Basil returned. They were in the company of other officers and civilians, so, therefore, used their proper names.

"I understand Mrs. Edwards would like to see me."

"Yes. I was surprised she didn't ask for her solicitor. Would you know why that is?"

"I can honestly say I do not," Ginger said. "Where is she?"

Basil led her to an interview room guarded by a young constable. Basil paused before opening the door. "Since you are not a solicitor and have no obligation for confidentiality, I shall require that you assist police efforts with anything she may bring to light."

"I thought she was already under arrest."

"Yes, but a jury shall decide her guilt. All evidence must be brought forward to prove her guilt or innocence."

"I understand."

Mrs. Edwards sat at a small table, hands threaded together on her lap. She scowled at Basil who had opened the door for Ginger.

Ginger sat on the chair facing the tense lady. When Basil left, closing the door firmly behind him, she said, "I understand you wanted to see me."

"It might be a mistake, seeing that you're in cahoots with the likes of him."

"I'm not sure what your intentions are."

"You're a private detective, aren't you?"

"I have been known to investigate for people who, for various reasons, don't want the police involved, or conversely, think I could assist the police."

Mrs. Edwards sighed long and hard. "I want to hire you."

"I see. To do what, exactly?"

"Find out who killed my husband."

"Are you saying you didn't kill him?"

Esme slapped the table. "I certainly did not. It's not like I hadn't dreamed about it, but I'm no killer, Lady Gold. See, I wouldn't mind hanging if I did it, but I don't mean to hang for someone else's crime. Lose my head without so much as a thank you?" She scoffed with indignation.

"Why do you think someone would want to kill Mr. Edwards?" Ginger asked.

"He was a louse. A philanderer." She nodded her head slowly and with meaning. "Liked the younger ones."

"Do you mean Miss Bertram and Miss Howard?"

"Them and others. I stopped keeping track."

"Why is that?"

"It's not like I could stop him. Besides, it kept him out of my bed."

"Who else knows about Mr. Edwards' proclivities?"

"His pro-what?"

"Your husband's extramarital affairs?"

"Oh, I don't know. He worked hard to keep it secret. The church, of course, frowns on such things, and he did love directing the choir."

"Mrs. Edwards, I need you to tell me exactly what happened the night your husband fell."

Esme Edwards' eyebrows formed a V. "You were there. You know what happened. Besides, I already told you and that inspector what I know."

"It would help me to hear it again from your point of view."

"Well, all right then." Mrs. Edwards leaned back and folded her arms. "I was playing the organ for the choir, and Theo kept turning around to scowl at me. He thought he was something when he directed the choir, like he had control or something. I mean, he's just getting a few people to sing, for crying out loud."

"And?" Ginger prompted.

"He was giving me these dirty looks, and it made me

angry, so I just pounded on the keys and the foot pedals even harder, just to spite him. I know it sounded like monkeys fighting in the jungle, but I didn't care. He stopped the singing and called for a break. He was up those steps before I could move my skirts and get away."

"Then what happened?"

"We had words, I can tell you. Nasty ones. And then I went down the stairs to use the ladies. But I swear he was alive when I left him, Lady Gold. I swear."

HALEY HAD a summer internship working in the mortuary at the Heart Hospital in Marylebone. The staff was familiar with Ginger as she often visited Haley there, especially when on a case. She made her way down to the cellar where the well-lit mortuary was located and tapped on the door to announce her presence,

"Hi, there," Haley said. "What brings you here? Besides my broad, beautiful face."

"Your broad, beautiful face is reason enough," Ginger said cheerily. "Don't you agree, Dr. Gupta?"

Dr. Manu Gupta grinned. He'd recently brought a bride back from India whom Ginger and Haley both agreed was simply adorable. It made being friends with the handsome doctor easier, having become equally acquainted with his new wife.

"Please finish up here, Miss Higgins," Dr. Gupta said. "I'll be in my office doing the paperwork."

"Actually, I have news," Ginger said as she watched Haley cover a corpse with a sheet and push the trolley into one of the cold cabinets. "Mrs. Edwards has been arrested on suspicion of murdering her husband."

"That was quick," Haley said. "I like the nice and tidy ones."

"Except that Mrs. Edwards denies it—adamantly. She's hired me to investigate."

Haley's dark brow reached for the ceiling. "Is that so. Do you believe her?"

"I think I do."

Haley locked the cabinet and filed the key in the pocket of her tweed skirt. "What did she tell you?"

Ginger related the conversation she'd had in the interview room at Scotland Yard.

"Not exactly a grieving widow," Haley said. "And with good reason, it seems. I can confirm that Theo Edwards had engaged in an intimate act earlier that day, but I'm afraid I couldn't tell you with whom."

"Someone present at Thursday night's choir rehearsal is our murderer." Ginger twisted a short strand of red hair around her finger. "I wish there were a way to tell if it was premeditated or an impulse killing. I did notice the door to the balcony near the vestry had recently been oiled. I'll have to have a word with Mr. Simpson about that."

"Have you narrowed down a list of suspects at all?" Haley asked.

Ginger motioned to a blackboard that hung on one wall. "May I?"

"By all means."

Ginger listed the names of all the people at the rehearsal who were without alibis on the night in question. "There's Miss Howard. She admitted to being in love with Theo Edwards."

Haley leaned against a table and folded her arms. "Perhaps she was the victim's assignation?"

Ginger tapped the tip of her chalk piece beside Marjorie Bertram's name. "Miss Bertram admitted that Mr. Edwards had been making romantic advances toward her, and though she tried to contain her emotions, became visibly upset about that."

She underlined Catherine Edwards. "Miss Edwards, the victim's sister. She seemed devoted to her brother, but perhaps she held a grievance."

Haley pushed a flyaway curl off her face. "Maybe she didn't like his affairs with the younger women."

"That's something to consider," Ginger agreed. "Miss Edwards doesn't appear overly fond of her sister-in-law, but that doesn't mean she'd condoned adultery."

The last name on the list was Cecil Piper.

"Mr. Piper is our least likely suspect," Ginger said.

"Those are the ones that often end up being guilty," Haley said.

"True. He didn't care for the way Mr. Edwards treated his wife. He might've struck out to protect her honour."

"What about the sexton? Did he have a grievance against the victim?" Haley asked.

"I wish I knew," Ginger said as she wrote Mr. Simpson's name on the board. "I'll have to ask Oliver about him."

"Is that all?" Haley asked.

Ginger pursed her lips as she considered something

distasteful. "There's Mary Blythe. She arrived just after the body fell. She could've run down from the balcony level."

"Was she out of breath?"

"I didn't notice."

"What motive would she have had?"

"Well," Ginger said as she added Mary's name to the list. "She's also a young, pretty girl. Theo Edwards would've noticed."

Haley grimaced. "Poor Reverend Hill."

"I'd like to start by interviewing Miss Howard," Ginger said. "I'm sure she'd have insight as to Mr. Edwards' character."

"And possibly inadvertently confess?" Haley added.

Ginger scoffed. "Wouldn't that be nice? I don't suppose you could come along?"

"Why not?" Haley pushed away from the table and smoothed out her tweed skirt. "I don't live here."

"One couldn't tell. Are you sure Dr. Gupta wouldn't mind?"

"It's slow at the moment. I'm due for a break, I should think." Haley retrieved her matching tweed jacket and black handbag. She pulled a face. "I'm assuming you drove the Crossley here?"

"I did."

"We could take a taxicab?" Haley said, hopefully.

"Nonsense! The Crossley has petrol and is ready to go."

They'd hardly been in the motorcar a minute before Haley grabbed onto the ceiling handle above the passenger window.

"Oh, Haley," Ginger said with a grin, "it's not that bad."

At that exact moment, a black cat dashed in front of the motorcar and Ginger swerved, nearly hitting the pavement, but managing to correct herself in time.

"Holy moly! Ginger, I swear, I'm never driving with you anywhere again."

"It's not my fault a black cat crossed my path. As they say in America, it's bad luck."

"You're not superstitious, are you?"

"Not usually. Except when a black cat crosses my path, and my good friend threatens to disown me."

"I hardly said I would disown you! Just your motor-car." Haley's eyes left the road for a split second to glare at Ginger. "When you're the driver."

Miss Anna Howard lived in a red-bricked terraced house in an area of London crowded with such houses. Ginger was glad she'd taken note of each suspect's personal address when Basil had asked the question during the interviews the night of the murder. She parked in front of the correct address.

An older lady with hair curlers tucked under a mesh scarf answered the doorbell. The lines around her mouth fanned out from pursed lips, and unruly eyebrows furrowed downwards. "We don't want any."

"Excuse me, madam," Ginger said quickly, not relishing the idea of the scarred wooden door slamming in their faces. "I'm Lady Gold, and this is Miss Higgins. We're here to see Miss Howard. Is she home?"

A younger voice called out from behind the lady. "Who is it, Mummy?"

"Friends of yours. A *la-dy*."

Anna Howard squealed and appeared from behind her mother. "Who is it?" Miss Howard had a white powdery substance on her nose and held up dough-encrusted fingers. Her expression switched from expectant to confused. "Oh."

"Hello, Miss Howard," Ginger said. "Would you mind if we came in. We just have a few questions about Mr. Edwards."

Mrs. Howard frowned. "What would my Anna know about a Mr. Edwards? She's not friendly with men."

"Mummy, that's the choir director from St. George's who died," Anna said. "I was there, remember. These ladies just want to chat about him. She waved a flour-covered palm. "Come into the kitchen. I'm baking some pies."

Ginger cast a glance at Haley. For a girl who'd recently professed love for the deceased, she seemed overly cheery.

Ginger and Haley each took a seat at the table.

"It smells fantastic in here," Haley said. "What kind of pies are you baking?"

"Chicken and leek. Can I get you some tea?"

Ginger and Haley accepted, and Miss Howard set the kettle to boil. "I hope you don't mind if I work whilst we talk," she said. "The oven's hot, and I don't like to waste the heat."

"Go ahead," Ginger said. "Like I mentioned earlier,

we'd like to ask a couple questions about your relation-ship with Theo Edwards."

Anna Howard's blonde head snapped up, her eyes on the kitchen door. She hurried to shut it while whispering over her shoulder. "I don't want my mum to hear. She'd be so disappointed in me if she knew."

"Forgive me for saying," Haley said, "but you don't seem overly upset."

Anna returned to her piecrust and began rolling.

"I am, actually. Heartbroken, if you must know. It's why I'm baking all these pies. If I don't keep busy, I'm a puddle, and Mummy would know. I just can't have that."

Ginger wondered just how far Anna Howard would go to keep her mother from discovering the truth.

Anna ran the top of her hand under her nose leaving a distracting flour moustache in its wake. The whistle blew, and Anna quickly brought out teacups, saucers, sugar, and milk along with the kettle and teapot.

"Do you mind pouring for yourself?" she asked. "My hands are slippery.

"How long had you been . . . meeting with Mr. Edwards?" Ginger asked as she poured for herself and Haley.

"About three weeks."

Haley raised a dark brow. "That seems like a short time to fall in love."

Anna's rolling pin stilled, and she stared, her eyes glis-tening. "When you know, you know. Theo and I were meant to be together."

A sob escaped Anna's throat, and she began to roll the

dough ferociously. "We were going to run away, you know. His wife didn't understand him. He said she was stark raving mad." She pointed the rolling pin at her guests. "She *was* mad, wasn't she? She killed her own husband!"

"She allegedly killed her husband," Ginger said gently. "She's innocent until proven guilty."

Anna sniffed. "Well, it's only a matter of time, then, isn't it? She's ruined everything, you know." Anna lowered her voice. "We were going to run away together, go to America where no one would know us. No one would know—"

"That he was already married to someone else?" Haley asked.

"I told you, that marriage was a sham. There weren't even any children! Theo said the marriage hadn't even been consummated."

Anna Howard's naïveté was stunning. It amazed Ginger how disillusioned one could be. Mr. Edwards was apparently a great deceiver and manipulator.

"I know you disapprove, that you think I'm an adulteress, and that I'm going to hell, but I don't care. I would've finally got out from under Mummy's thumb. Now . . ." Her voice drifted off, and she hiccupped.

"Did Mrs. Edwards know about your affair?" Haley asked.

Anna shook her head. "It wasn't an affair. They didn't even sleep in the same room. Mrs. Edwards slept in Catherine's room."

Ginger shared a knowing look with Haley. The poor girl was deluded.

"To your knowledge, Miss Howard," Ginger started, "did Mrs. Edwards know about your relationship with Mr. Edwards."

Anna sighed. "To my knowledge, no. No one knew. Theo said we had to keep it totally secret to protect my reputation. He was so thoughtful that way. Now if you don't mind, I really need to take care of my pies, or they're bound to flop."

"Thank you for the tea," Ginger said.

Mrs. Howard was seated in a rocking chair in the living room. Ginger smiled as they passed through, but the elder Howard lady stared back with a look of suspicion.

Ginger opened the door and nearly ran into the knuckles of the next guest about to knock.

Basil Reed's mouth spread into a grin. "Hello, Ginger. Hello, Miss Higgins." Then to Ginger, he said, "Why am I not surprised to see you here?"

"As you already know," Ginger answered haughtily, "Mrs. Edwards has employed me to look into this case."

"Yes. She's quite vocal about her innocence," Basil said.

"Perhaps that's because she *is* innocent."

"Perhaps."

Mrs. Howard shuffled up behind them. "Come or go, but don't stand there with the door open!"

"Sorry, Mrs. Howard," Ginger said. "Miss Higgins and I were just leaving, but there's someone else here to see you."

Mrs. Howard gave Basil a withering look. "Whatever you're selling, young man, we don't want any!"

GINGER SLID into the driver's seat of her motorcar. Haley opened her door but hesitated.

"Are you going to get in?" Ginger asked.

"I think there's a bus stop near here."

"Don't tell me you're so frightened of the Crossley that you'd rather take the bus."

"I'm not frightened of the Crossley, I'm frightened with *you* driving the Crossley."

"I'm going to visit Miss Bertram. Surely, you want to join me?"

"I do."

"Then get in."

"Fine," Haley muttered as she settled in and shut the passenger door. "But if I die at your hands, I promise I'll come back to haunt you."

Ginger laughed. "Deal."

Miss Marjorie Bertram lived in a flat in a stone and brick house that had once been lived in by a wealthy family but had now been divided into several smaller abodes. Miss Bertram responded to the ringing of the bell of her ground-floor flat.

"He was right," she said on seeing them. "Come on in."

Ginger stared at the youthful, sensible brunette.

"Hello, Miss Bertram. What do you mean, he was right?"

"Chief Inspector Reed. He said there was a good

chance that you might call around."

"He did, did he?" Ginger said through tight lips. "What else did he say?"

"That I was to cooperate and answer your questions."

Ginger glanced sideways at Haley who merely shrugged.

"Would you like some tea?"

"That would be splendid," Ginger said.

Haley whispered in Ginger's ear. "More tea? I'm going to float away."

The sitting room was brightly decorated with a light, paisley-print wallpaper; whitewashed floor with a large wool rug; and rose pin-cushion chairs placed in a semi-circle around a fireplace, now lit. Above the mantelpiece was a photograph in a circular frame of a lady wearing a red dress.

"Do you live alone, Miss Bertram?" Haley asked.

"No. I have a flatmate, Charlotte, but she's at work. She's a nurse at the hospital. Works all sorts of hours, so I never know when she'll be around. It's nice, though. I like being alone."

"Are you employed?" Ginger asked.

"I'm a typist."

After asking how Ginger and Haley liked their tea, Marjorie Bertram poured three cups. She settled in her chair and picked up a partially completed doily made of fine white cotton stabbed with a narrow crochet hook.

"You don't mind if I crochet while we talk?" she asked.

"Of course not," Ginger said. "You do lovely work."

"Thank you, Lady Gold. I find crocheting helps me to

relax. With everything that's happened . . . Well, this is my second since . . ."

"Yes," Ginger said, helping her along. "Mr. Edwards' death was quite tragic."

Miss Bertram worked her crochet hook furiously. "I've never seen a dead body before. Charlotte has, of course, and thinks I'm making too much of it."

"I recall feeling very distressed by my first dead body," Haley said.

Miss Bertram paused and stared. "Your *first*?"

"Miss Higgins is training to become a pathologist," Ginger explained. When Miss Bertram's eyes failed to register understanding, Ginger continued. "A pathologist examines bodies for cause of death."

Miss Bertram's mouth dropped open. "Why on earth would you want a job like that?"

"It can be quite interesting," Haley said. "Especially when a postmortem exam helps to solve a crime. Prove criminal intent. Forensic science is useful in proving guilt and innocence."

Miss Bertram returned to her crocheting with fervour. "To each their own, I suppose. You and Charlotte would certainly have something to talk about."

"Miss Bertram, you told me on Thursday that Mr. Edwards had made unwanted advances, but you turned him down."

Miss Bertram's pale face flushed red with embarrassment and her hands stilled.

"That's correct. But I told him in no uncertain terms that I wasn't interested. He was a bore, and tricked other, stupid girls, but I wasn't one of them. And I certainly didn't kill him over it."

"No one is suggesting that you did," Ginger said.

Miss Bertram laid her crochet down on the coffee table. "Then why are you here?"

"We're trying to find the truth. You never know what small piece of information can lead to it."

"I've already told the police, and now you—twice—everything I know." She stood, indicating her wish to end the interview.

"Thank you for your time," Ginger said as she and Haley rose to their feet. "We'll see ourselves out."

"Well, what do you think of that?" Haley asked once they were safely out of earshot.

"I find it interesting what people do to relax in times of stress. Miss Howard bakes pies, Miss Bertram crochets."

"You shop," Haley said.

Ginger stared back at her friend. "I suppose I do. And you?"

"I read medical textbooks."

Ginger grinned.

Haley opened the passenger door but didn't get in. "I think Miss Bertram's hiding something."

"Possibly," Ginger said. "The question is what?"

"Maybe she knows who did it and wants to protect that person."

"Or perhaps she's the killer. Are you getting in?"

Haley wrinkled her nose and shook her head. "Nah. I'll take the bus. I want to live to see another day."

# CHAPTER FIFTEEN

Ginger parked the Crossley in the stone garage and made a detour to the stables to visit Goldmine, her Akhal-Teke gelding. The breed was rare in England, an import from Turkmenistan, and known for its glossy, silky hair. Ginger never failed to get lingering, inquisitive gazes when she took Goldmine out for a ride, and not only because she was a woman riding astride.

Unsurprisingly, she found Scout there, smelling of oats, hay, and horse sweat. He was brushing the animal's golden coat.

"H-ello, missus," he said with a toothy smile. "Come to ride Goldmine, have ya?"

Ginger wrinkled her nose guiltily. "I'm afraid not. I don't have time today." In fact, she needed to start getting ready for another dinner engagement with William. "Would you like to ride him?"

Scout's pointy chin dropped in surprise. "On my own?"

Like most street children, the lad hadn't had an opportunity to learn to ride before staying with Ginger at Hartigan House. She'd given him a few lessons, but he wasn't ready to take the horse out on his own.

"How about I ask Mr. Clement to lead you around?"

Scout's bright eyes beamed up at her. "That would be grand, missus."

Ginger found Clement raking dead leaves in the garden and arranged for him to assist Scout. She'd only just entered the house through the French windows when she heard a distressed voice.

"You can't leave me!"

Ginger recognised it immediately as belonging to Louisa and wondered why she was already home from Feathers & Flair.

Felicia, wearing a yellow rayon day dress and a look of indifference, passed Ginger in the passage as she carried a book to the sitting room.

"What's wrong with Louisa?" Ginger asked.

Felicia shrugged. "When is something *not* wrong with Louisa?"

Ginger braced herself as she headed to the staircase. Louisa and her maid were having words on the landing.

"Ginger!" Louisa said when she spotted her half-sister heading upstairs. "Jenny is going back to Boston."

Louisa's bedraggled-looking maid stood with her hands clasped and her chin drooping.

"Jenny," Ginger said when she reached them. "Are you unhappy here?"

Louisa answered for her. "She says she's homesick."

"I miss my family, ma'am," Jenny said. She was dressed in a brown jacket and a straw hat, and her grey eyes were full of determination.

Ginger's gaze landed on the worn leather suitcase. "Are you leaving right now?"

"Just to Liverpool, then on to Boston tomorrow."

"It does seem rather sudden," Ginger stated.

Jenny's eyes drifted to Louisa and back to the floor, and Ginger understood. Louisa's demanding and ungrateful manner had caused more than one maid to seek employment elsewhere.

Ginger turned to her sister. "Perhaps it's time for you to go home too. Jenny can chaperone."

"I'm not leaving London *right now*."

"I'm sure Jenny would be willing to delay her travel plans." To Jenny, she added quickly, "You'd be properly compensated, of course."

Louisa folded her arms over a new Madeleine Vionnet frock Ginger recognised from her shop—a red silk crepe Georgette with gold piping trim and a matching attached scarf—and stomped her red T-strap sandal. "I'm not leaving."

"Well then, I suppose you must say goodbye."

"But I'll have no maid," Louisa whined.

"I'm sure Grace and Lizzie can provide whatever help you need. You are quite able-bodied yourself, you know."

"What is all this commotion about?" Ambrosia stuck

her head out from the drawing room and stared up at the second-floor landing. She must've been napping in her wing-backed chair as her newly styled bob was flattened on one side. She'd be mortified if she knew and would spew further regrets about having her Victorian-style bun cut off.

"Sorry, Grandmother," Ginger said. "We'll take this into another room."

Jenny bobbed. "If you'll excuse me. I have a train to catch. Farewell, Miss Hartigan."

Ginger and Louisa watched in silence as Jenny scampered down the staircase and disappeared on her way to the green baize door.

Louisa groaned. "It's so hard to find loyal help."

"You might like to try being more agreeable."

"*I am* agreeable."

"Shouldn't you be at work? Why aren't you at Feathers & Flair?"

"It got awfully dull after a while. I don't know how Dora and Emily do it."

"It's Dorothy and Emma," Ginger said incredulously.

"Oh, well, yes," Louisa said with a dismissive wave. "Anyway, Madame Roux said I could leave."

Oh, mercy. Ginger feared her shop manager was unhappy with Ginger's latest employee.

"Did you at least bring Boss home with you?" Ginger had a dreadful notion that she would have to turn around to retrieve him.

"Of course. I'm not that irresponsible. He's in your room."

"Fabulous."

Before Ginger could make her way there, Pippins approached the bottom of the stairs with a silver platter in one hand. On it was a white envelope.

"The afternoon post, madam," he said. "It's for Miss Hartigan."

Louisa was already halfway down the stairs when Pippins said her name, and she hurried down the rest of the way to meet him. Her smile of anticipation dropped when she read the name of the sender.

"Who's it from?" Ginger asked.

Louisa carried it up the stairs as she thumbed it open. "Mama. I don't know if I can bear to read it." She handed it to Ginger. "It's always the same thing. Her pleading for me to come back."

"It's not too late to fetch Jenny."

"No! I can't give in to Mama until she learns her lesson."

Ginger stared at Louisa, alarmed. "Her lesson?"

"She has to stop bossing me around."

"Louisa, she's your mother. She cares about your well-being. You can't fault her for that."

Louisa snatched the letter from Ginger's fingers. "I see that you are on her side." She stormed to her room and slammed the door.

Oh, mercy!

Something would have to be done about Louisa and her bad temperament, but Ginger didn't have time to deal with her now.

Boss jumped off the bed when he heard Ginger come

in, stretched out his legs, yawned, then pranced to Ginger's side. She scooped him up.

"Dear Bossy. I'm sorry for leaving you with my spoiled little sister."

GINGER'S BEDROOM was large and decorated with gold and ivory trim. A full-length ornately trimmed mirror stood in the corner near a matching dressing table, while two striped ivory and gold chairs sat in front of the long windows. The bed featured prominently against one wall with extravagantly carved wood head and footboards. She and Daniel had stayed in this room when they visited London on their wedding journey in 1913, and for the first few months after returning to live at Hartigan House, she couldn't be in this room without having vivid memories of him.

Kindly, those memories had faded, and the black-and-white photo of her husband in uniform had once again been safely tucked away into the bedside table drawer.

Ginger swung open her wardrobe doors.

"So, Bossy. What shall I wear?"

Ginger thumbed through the dresses that hung neatly on the rod. Her significant inheritance, along with being the owner of a high-quality retail dress shop had its advantages. Ginger's collection of dresses was awe-inspiring. All the great designers were represented: Edward Molyneux, Jeanne Lanvin, the Callot Sisters, Lucile, and others.

William was picking her up at seven o'clock, so she

only had an hour and a half to prepare. Hardly enough time, once a bath was factored into the equation, and Ginger had most definitely factored it in. She certainly didn't want to smell like Anna Howard's chicken and leek pie. At that very moment, Lizzie was preparing the bath. Ginger had instructed her to put extra lavender in it.

Ginger turned the key in the bathroom door to ensure her privacy—Louisa wasn't known to knock— padded across the black-and-white tiled floor, dropped her negligée on the thick yellow bath mat, and slipped into the steamy water that filled the white claw-foot tub.

Sinking down deep, she let out a satisfied sigh. She closed her eyes intending to clear her mind, but the noise of the case just grew louder. There was no sense fighting it, and perhaps she'd think of something vital.

Miss Howard, Miss Bertram, Miss Edwards, or Mr. Piper could have raced up to the balcony after Theo Edwards had gone up to chastise his wife. Or the killer had been already up there waiting, which would leave Mrs. Edwards, Mr. Simpson, and Miss Blythe. But how could they have known Mr. Edwards would call for a break during the choir rehearsal and go up? Unless it was a crime of opportunity. Mrs. Edwards was already there. Mr. Simpson could've been doing some cleaning. Mary Blythe might've gone up just to observe.

The murderer either planned in advance or acted in a bout of passion—removed the pipe from the organ, hit Theo Edwards in the temple, and either pushed or watched him fall to the pews below, returned the weapon to its position in the organ, then joined the rest of the group and expressed shock and horror at the presumed accident, or alleged crime.

Ginger let her mind go over all the suspects and the interviews, but even in her state of relaxation, her unconscious mind unlocked no new clues.

She drowsed a little before becoming aware of the cooling water.

"Oh mercy," she said splashing water as she got to her feet and grabbed her towel. "I'm going to be late!"

Back in her room, she chose one of her favourite dresses, a lime-green satin Callot Soeurs. Sleeveless with a V-shaped collar trimmed in soft pink lace. Large pink embroidered circles started at the waist with the skirt losing the green hue. The hem was detailed with inverted arches and long pink tassels hanging from the points.

"What do you think?" she asked Boss as she twirled in front of the mirror. Boss was mid-stretch on the top of Ginger's bed, his small behind and stub of a tail high in the air. He yawned and lay down again, looking rather like one of those stone lions at the corners of Nelson's Column on Trafalgar Square.

"It's too last season, isn't it?" Ginger asked, acknowledging Boss' yawn. She took another look, back and front. "Oh, it is, isn't it? But I just love how it looks!"

Ginger checked her watch. "Perhaps the latest from Molyneux." She examined a black satin frock heavily embroidered with gold leaf. "I might have time to change if I hurry."

Ginger didn't know why she was so concerned about dressing for William. He loved her no matter what she wore. She could wear a potato sack, and he'd still find her adorable.

Before Ginger could wiggle out of the Callot, the doorbell resounded through the entrance hall and along the high ceilings to the second floor.

"Oh, drat. He's early." Ginger quickly straightened the tunic of the Callot frock, checked her makeup in the mirror—narrowly trimmed eyebrows over smoky-blue shadow on her eyelids; circles of rouge on her cheeks, and glossy red lipstick on her lips—and added one squirt of *Parfum de Coty*. She paused to take a breath. Lizzie peeked in. "There's a gentleman here for you, madam."

"Thank you, Lizzie. I'll be down shortly."

Ginger decided she mustn't look too eager. William was early, after all. He could wait. She thought about changing into the Molyneux but was too exhausted to do it. Instead, she played with Boss.

Five minutes later, Ginger sauntered down the stair-case, smile ready, when she suddenly froze. It wasn't William waiting for her, but *Basil*.

"What are *you* doing here?" She sped down the steps to face her visitor.

"I was in the area—"

"*Pfft*. You knew I was having dinner with William."

"Oh. Was that tonight?"

"Don't play coy with me."

Basil grinned. "I'm not. I honestly just dropped in to ask you how your interviews went today. I thought we could share notes."

Ginger cocked her head. "Why don't I believe you?"

Basil chuckled. "I'm not sure. You smell nice, by the way. I've always loved that dress on you."

Drat! She should've changed into her new Molyneux!

"You have to leave. William's going to be here any minute."

"Great. I'd love to chat with the good captain."

"You would *not*. I know you Basil Reed, and you just want to cause trouble."

"If that trouble is you, then you're correct."

Ginger stared indignantly.

"And," Basil continued. "You're right. You *do* know me."

"You are a brute."

"Thank you."

The doorbell chimed, and Ginger stiffened.

Pippins duly appeared. "Shall I get that for you, madam?"

"It's all right, Pips. I'm here. I'll get it."

"Very well." Pippins disappeared, which Ginger knew her kind butler would do. She didn't want him to witness what would undoubtedly prove to be an awkward situation.

"Hello, William," Ginger said. "The chief inspector was just leaving."

William's happy countenance darkened. "Hello, Chief Inspector."

Basil held out his hand. "Good to see you, old chap."

William shook Basil's hand with a look of reluctance. "What brings you here?" he asked.

Ginger thought William's question quite forward and

out of place. "We were discussing the case," she said, taking his arm.

Basil didn't take the hint and make his leave. "Oh yes. Lady Gold has a very clever brain for puzzles," he said. "A master at the crossword puzzle, too. Have you heard of this new craze? Apparently, the Americans are quite obsessed. I do believe one must have a vast assortment of knowledge to complete one of those correctly." He grinned condescendingly at the captain and continued, "I've found Ginger's deductive reasoning to be stellar in past cases and believe she shall find this challenging case no different."

Ginger felt herself blush at his praises. "You're overstating my capabilities, Chief Inspector."

"Hardly. Captain Beale, you must agree that Ginger is more than a pretty face."

William ruffled. "Of course."

"We met on the SS *Rosa*," Basil said. "Has Ginger mentioned it?"

"Yes," William admitted tersely.

"She convinced me then that a female presence in interviews would help to set the suspect at ease, and you know, she was right!" He locked his eyes on her. "I've wanted her at my side ever since."

Ginger's pulse pounded at the less-than-benign meaning. The romantic tension between them was palpable, and William Beale was in no way blind to it.

"Yes, well, very good," William said, pulling Ginger away. "Our reservation is waiting. Good day, Chief Inspector."

Basil waved them off. "Enjoy your meal."

"Well, that was darn awkward," William said as the taxicab pulled away. "Can't you do something to keep him at bay?"

"Why would I do that?"

"Because—"

"It's true we've worked on many cases together," Ginger said, hoping she sounded reassuring. "This is just another one. It's just work."

"Work is what one does when one is in financial need."

"One can work for a sense of satisfaction. A sense of purpose."

"But don't you have your dress shop for that? Why do you need to do this private investigator . . . thing? It's quite unbecoming for a lady."

Ginger gasped. "Is that what you really think?"

The captain had the good sense to look remorseful. "No, no, I'm sorry. It's just that Reed fellow gets my goat." He reached for Ginger's hand and stared deeply into her eyes. "He's after you."

Ginger couldn't deny it. Basil had admitted it himself.

William lifted her gloved hand to his lips and kissed it. "I don't want to lose you, Lady Gold."

William and Basil had both been ill-mannered in their behaviour the evening before, and Ginger hadn't enjoyed her dinner engagement with William at all, not even finishing her veal cutlets. Well, today she'd get by without seeing either of them. Dining with William was starting to become a habit, and Ginger felt it was too soon in their friendship to get into that kind of routine.

Tomorrow the King's ball, a rousing gala for the wealthy, was taking place at the Ritz ballroom. Ginger had promised William ages ago that she'd attend on his arm.

Ginger's mind snapped to the present at the sound of horns blasting at the crossroads where a police officer was impatiently waving her through. Sunday afternoon traffic was usually lighter with the shops closed, but churchgoers on their way home from services were making up the difference. Unfortunately, with the murder at St. George's, the services had to be cancelled. Ginger had attended the parish church in Kensington with Ambrosia and Felicia earlier.

"Patience, patience!" she said as she changed gears. She stepped on the accelerator and rumbled along just to get stuck behind a slower-moving horse-drawn cart.

"They really ought to have a separate lane for the animals," she said to Boss, who sat upright in the seat next to her, his nose propped on the open window. "It's one thing to have a motorcar repaired after a crash, but quite another to fix a horse, don't you think?"

Boss yipped in agreement, and Ginger reached over to tickle his head.

"We could walk faster than this," she muttered in frustration. Adjusting the rearview mirror, she used the time to reapply her lipstick. Finally, the driver of the cart turned onto a side road, and Ginger was able to pick up speed.

She was heading to Mary Blythe's house. She'd promised Oliver she'd have a word with Mary. She dearly hoped Mary had had a change of heart regarding being wed to Oliver and was only in need of a nudge of encouragement to follow through with her convictions.

The Blythe family was middle-class and lived in a small stone house with a middling garden guarded by an English springer spaniel. Ginger was making an assumption she'd find Mary at home—for she was unlikely to seek out a new church to attend whilst engaged to the vicar of another—and was grateful to be proven right.

Carrying Boss carefully past the docile Blythe family

pet, she knocked on the yellow door. Mary's eyes widened in surprise.

"Lady Gold?"

"Good afternoon, Miss Blythe. I hope I'm not disturbing you, but I'm wondering if you have time for a visit."

"Of course," Mary said politely.

"Is it all right if my dog comes inside? I'll keep him on my lap and out of harm's way. Otherwise, I can return him to my motorcar."

"It's fine. We're dog lovers here." Mary reached out to stroke Boss. "He's a dear little thing."

Mary left Ginger alone in a cosy and tidy parlour whilst she prepared the obligatory tea. The room still carried a morning chill, but Boss did his part to warm her by curling up on her lap.

In short order, Mary returned with a tea tray—she'd already had the kettle on—and set it on a tea table between them. Ginger couldn't help but notice the circles around Mary's dark eyes and gathered that she herself wasn't the only one suffering from lack of rest. Ginger felt a wave of pity for the bride-to-be and wondered if she was about to overstep by nosing into what, as Haley would have no problem pointing out, was none of her business.

Well, she was here now. At the very least, she could offer some comfort and commiserate with Mary in her misery.

"Are your parents home?" Ginger asked. With the

forthcoming conversation being of such a delicate nature, she didn't want to get interrupted.

"No. They've gone to have tea with my uncle and aunt."

Ginger took her first sip of tea, then asked, "How are you doing, Miss Blythe? It must be such a tremendous disappointment to have to postpone your wedding."

"Yes, it is. Dreadfully."

"But your love for Reverend Hill can weather the storm, I'm sure. It'll only be another two weeks or so, I gather?"

Ginger watched Mary's expression carefully.

Mary wrung thin hands. "I hope you are right."

Leaning towards Mary, Ginger smiled gently. "I hope it's not too forward of me to say, but you don't appear very happy. Are you sure this is what you want?"

Mary's eyes widened. "What do you mean?"

"Do you really want to marry Reverend Hill? Do you love him?"

Shock registered on Mary's face. "Oh, Lady Gold, you mustn't ask me such a thing."

Ginger sipped her tea, then said, "I believe you've answered my question. It's not too late, Miss Blythe. It's not too late to do the right thing."

Mary's eyes glistened with worry, and Ginger could almost see her wheels spin.

"No," she finally said. "I'm going to marry Oliver."

Ginger held in the sigh that she felt building, letting her breath out slowly and quietly. "Splendid. I'm sure it shall be a very happy day."

Mary forced a smile. "Is there anything else you'd like to talk about, Lady Gold?"

Ginger felt a tad embarrassed at having her motives for the visit being called out.

"Well, I suppose we'd be remiss if we didn't talk about what happened to poor Mr. Edwards. Not to bring up a sore point, Miss Blythe, but someone killed that man and wouldn't you feel better if his murderer was caught before you walked down the aisle?"

"Yes. Of course. But I don't know how I can help."

Stroking Boss languidly, Ginger casually asked, "How well did you know Mr. Edwards?"

Mary lifted her teacup and sipped, but Ginger couldn't help wonder if she was using it as a shield to hide her expression. "The same as most, I suppose."

"Had Mr. Edwards ever behaved in an unbecoming fashion towards you?"

Mary's hand shook so that the teacup rattled as she returned it to its saucer. "Why would you ask that?"

"It's come to my attention that other young ladies have complained about his being too forward with them— acting inappropriately for a married man."

Anna Howard hadn't exactly complained, Ginger thought, but she would've if she had any sense in her.

Mary blinked hard. "Is that so?"

"Yes."

"Maybe one of them killed him, then."

"They would have motive, certainly. Is there anyone else you can think of who might have motive?" *Like you, Miss Blythe?*

Mary stared hard then accepted the challenge.

"Mr. Piper was there. He and Mr. Edwards weren't on the best of terms."

"Do you know why?"

"I can only guess. It would be gossip for me to say."

"Do you think something was going on between Mrs. Edwards and Mr. Piper?"

Mary shrugged a thin shoulder. "I can't say."

"Because you don't know, or it isn't polite?" Ginger prodded.

"It's gossip, madam."

"It's a murder inquiry, Miss Blythe."

Mary jutted out her chin. "Mr. Piper works at the County Mental Hospital. Perhaps you should ask him."

# CHAPTER SEVENTEEN

Back in the Crossley, Boss sat upright in the passenger seat as Ginger retrieved her notebook from her handbag and looked up Cecil Piper's house address.

"Are you up for another motorcar ride, Boss?"

Boss' tongue was hanging loosely out of his mouth, his black lips curled upwards slightly giving the dog a look of perpetually smiling.

Ginger drove to Mr. Piper's boarding house near Guildhall, parked on the street, and reassured Boss she wouldn't be long. A disgruntled landlady wearing a stained apron answered Ginger's knock. Her deep-set eyes scanned Ginger suspiciously. "We only take gentleman lodgers 'ere. No lady visitors allowed."

"I'm Lady Gold," Ginger said, hoping the use of her title would soften the lady's demeanour. It often did, but not in this case.

"Like I said, no lady visitors."

Ginger smiled and tried again. "I'm a private investigator, looking for Mr. Cecil Piper."

"A private wot?"

"Investigator. I have questions for Mr. Piper."

"Well, 'e ain't 'ere. Fankfully, 'e's one of the ones wiv a job."

The landlady rudely closed the door in Ginger's face without so much as a goodbye.

Ginger had hoped Mr. Piper would have had the day off, but mental institutions didn't shut down on Sundays and somebody had to work there. Now she'd have to make a trip out to the country. It was a good forty-five-minute drive to the County Mental Hospital, a long way to go to work every day. Surely, Mr. Piper could find lodgings a little closer. Perhaps there was a good train connection.

Whatever his reasons for living in this particular boarding house, it meant that Ginger had to drive out to the outskirts of the west end of London if she wanted to try to track him down there. Ginger dropped Boss off at Hartigan House before heading back on the road and out of the city.

The County Mental Hospital was like a small town of its own, with a church steeple jutting into the sky amongst a cluster of stone and brick buildings ranging in height from one to three storeys. The grounds sloped gently eastward towards the River Brent, north of the Grand Union Canal. Ginger drove along Uxbridge Road until she reached the Windmill Lane junction. Finding Mr. Piper would be trickier than Ginger had hoped. She didn't even know what part of the hospital he worked in.

A long cobbled driveway led to the main gate and happily to an office. What she hadn't expected to see there, though Ginger was beginning to believe the fates were working against her, was the sight of a forest-green Austin 7, and the man in a crisp suit and trilby hat exiting it.

Basil turned towards the sound of Ginger's motorcar, and a debonair grin slowly crossed his face. His eyes lingered on Ginger as she exited her motorcar, one stockinged leg at a time—how else was one to extract oneself? The skirt of her lavender silk and crepe frock fluttered in the breeze, and Ginger was keenly aware of how the fabric pressed against her figure. Basil's hazel eyes locked onto hers, and her stomach flipped, flopped, and flipped again.

Drat, the man!

With her shoulders back and her head—sporting a purple felt hat adorned with a white feather—held high, Ginger approached and said in greeting, "It seems great minds think alike, Chief Inspector."

"Indeed. Am I to assume you are visiting an ailing relative, or are you, once again, getting in the way of police business?"

"I'm here in my own official capacity," Ginger said, jutting her chin up. "As you well know, Mrs. Edwards has hired me to look into this case for her. Not that she doesn't trust the police to do their jobs, I'm sure."

"Perhaps we should proceed as colleagues and not as competitors."

Ginger's brow arched inquisitively. "Are you suggesting we share information?"

"I do believe you've been making your own enquiries, and it would seem most expedient, don't you think?"

"I'm sure you're right," Ginger said.

"Ladies first."

"Very well, Miss Blythe informed me that Mr. Piper was employed at this hospital," Ginger said. "I confess I didn't know his profession before then."

"Yes, but not really a case-solving revelation. Since, well, I'm already here."

Ginger ignored his playful jab. "No, but she also insinuated that he and Mrs. Edwards had a relationship of some sort."

Basil raised a brow. "Romantic? Isn't she rather, ahem, old for him?"

"Not necessarily romantic, and beauty lies in the eyes of the beholder. Your turn."

"Apparently Mrs. Edwards did or does have an ailing relative here."

"Is that so?" Ginger said. "Do you know who?"

"I can only speculate."

"Shall we visit Mr. Piper together or separately?"

"We're both here; we might as well go in together," Basil said. "Besides," he added with a twinkle in his eye, "my credentials may actually get us in the door."

Ginger scowled, wanting to protest, but alas, he was right.

Inside the office, a man in a cheap suit staffed the desk. Police identification often worked like a magic wand. At first, the man blocked their request to enter by asking for proof of relationship and permission from said patient's physician. Ginger had neither of these and would've been put out on her ear had she not had Basil Reed at her side. She bristled at the idea that Basil was *necessary*, but she had to admit, at times, it was handy having him around.

The grounds of the mental hospital were in need of cleaning and trimming. The war had taken many of the male workers, and, it appeared that only the basic needs were being covered now. The village feel was further tainted by the lack of normal, healthy inhabitants. Patients were often listless, their eyes lifeless, as staff walked with them for exercise and fresh air.

They found Mr. Piper walking with one of these patients, an overly slim middle-aged man in trousers and a spring coat that no longer fitted him properly.

Mr. Piper's jaw tightened on seeing Ginger and Basil approaching. No doubt, they were the last folks he thought he'd encounter at work today.

"Lady Gold and Chief Inspector Reed, what are you doing here?"

"We've come to see you, Mr. Piper," Basil answered. "We've questions for you about Mr. Edwards."

"Very well," Mr. Piper said, looking rather displeased. He called for another attendant who took Mr. Piper's charge and headed indoors.

They came to an empty wooden bench in need of a

coat of paint. Ginger and Mr. Piper sat whilst Basil elected to remain standing.

"I'm not sure how I can help," Mr. Piper said. He clasped his hands tightly in his lap. "I don't really know anything."

Ginger knew that was untrue and shared a look with Basil. Why had Mr. Piper started off their query with a lie?

"It's our understanding that the Edwards', particularly Mrs. Edwards, frequented the County Mental Hospital," Basil said. "You must've seen them when they were visiting?"

"As you can see, this hospital is rather large."

Basil pressed the matter. "Did you see them?"

"Well, yes, as a matter of fact. In a professional manner, of course."

"Who were they visiting?" Ginger asked.

"Oh, I can't say," Mr. Piper said quickly. "Patient confidentiality."

"Might I remind you that this is a murder investigation, Mr. Piper," Basil said. "Your failure to cooperate doesn't look good."

Basil's insinuation stunned the attendant. "What do you mean? No, wait. *I'm* a suspect?"

"Everyone who was on the premises of St. George's Church and not in the nave when Mr. Edwards fell to his death is a suspect," Basil explained. "So, would you like to try again?"

Mr. Piper's gaze moved from Basil to Ginger, his eyes

flashing with indecision. Finally, he said, "It was Miss Catherine Edwards."

Ginger was stunned by his pronouncement. Catherine Edwards showed standard signs of grief now, and before her brother died, she'd seemed happy and settled.

"What was her diagnosis?" Ginger asked.

"Melancholia. Normally, our patients show signs of improvement after some weeks in our care, and Miss Edwards was typical in this regard until she had a crisis and begged her brother to take her home. Against the doctor's strong advice that she stay. New advances in medicine happen all the time, but Theo Edwards discharged her anyway."

"Perhaps Catherine was bright enough to not want to be a guinea pig of sorts," Ginger said.

Mr. Piper frowned at the inference but said nothing.

"How close are you to Mrs. Edwards?" Basil asked.

Mr. Piper's forehead began to glisten with sweat. "Not at all."

"You're saying that you and Mrs. Edwards *weren't* friendly," Ginger said.

"I suppose you could say we are friends, but nothing romantic."

Ginger thought he sounded rueful.

"But you would've like to?" she asked gently.

Mr. Piper looked taken aback. "Not at all. Besides, she was married and for whatever reason, intended to stand by her husband, no matter his behaviour."

"That made you angry, didn't it?" Basil said.

"He was a cad."

"She's free to marry now," Basil pushed. "Once the grieving period is over."

"Except for the fact that she's in prison," Mr. Piper said.

Ginger wondered if she had it all wrong. Maybe Mr. Piper's motive wasn't to free Mrs. Edwards but to *punish* her.

"Whatever you are thinking," Mr. Piper said indignantly, "I'm not interested in Mrs. Edwards. Not then and not now."

# CHAPTER EIGHTEEN

The next day Ginger decided to make a stop at St. George's Church to speak to Mr. Simpson. A short while later, she pulled into the churchyard, adjusted her cloche hat, and stepped out. With Boss in her arms, she searched the church for Oliver and, not finding him, looked for Mrs. Davies. The secretary was busy in the kitchen, but happy to take a break to chat.

"Oh, Reverend Hill is visiting Mrs. Childs. She's ill in bed now, poor thing. Doesn't look like she has long in this world. It's good for the reverend to be serving others right now. Keep his mind off his own troubles, you know."

"That is the truth," Ginger said. "Mrs. Davies, do you know where I would find Mr. Simpson?"

"I believe he's weeding the graveyard. Is there something I can help you with?"

"No. I just have a question or two to ask him, then I must be off."

"No time for tea?"

Ginger smiled. "Not this time, Mrs. Davies, but soon, I promise."

In the graveyard, Ginger lowered Boss to the ground and let him chase butterflies. She spotted Mr. Simpson looking like a large grasshopper, with his long legs bent at sharp angles on the grass, his grey head hidden at first by a lopsided gravestone. Ginger held in a smile.

"Mr. Simpson?"

The sexton sat back on his heels and stared up at Ginger with a questioning gaze. Ginger had the feeling that people didn't often talk to the caretaker, that he was more of a shadow and a silent partner to the parishioners of St. George's Church.

He brushed off bits of grass as he slowly straightened to a standing position, long fingers pushing at the small of his back.

"Lady Gold?" he asked simply.

"I'm sorry to bother you," Ginger said. "Fine work, by the way. I believe weeding is a thankless job."

"I don't mind it, madam."

"Good. Can I ask you a couple of questions regarding the tragic event that just occurred at the church?"

Mr. Simpson nodded.

"Did you know Mr. Edwards?"

"I know everyone who serves at the church, madam. It's my business to know. I have the keys, and I make sure things are clean and ready for Sunday services."

"Yes, but did you know Mr. Edwards on a personal level."

"No, madam."

The sexton didn't even blink, and Ginger found herself believing him.

"Just one more thing. The stairwell door by the vestry leading to the balcony, did you oil it recently?"

"Yes, madam. It's my job to make sure the doors and windows work properly."

"Very good, Mr. Simpson. Thank you for your time."

Ginger called for Boss, leaving a bewildered-looking Mr. Simpson and returned to her motorcar feeling quite disturbed. She was no closer to finding the killer or discovering if the murder had been premeditated or not.

Ginger was pleased to find Haley home that afternoon.

"The hospital has set you free?"

"I did an early morning shift," Haley explained.

"Join me for tea in the sitting room?" Ginger asked. She always found discussing a perplexing case with her intelligent friend quite helpful.

"Make it coffee and you have a deal."

Ginger arranged for Lizzie to prepare a tea tray with tea for her and coffee for Haley. Throwing off her shoes, she put her feet up on the ottoman. Boss curled up on her lap and started snoring. If only she could fall asleep so quickly!

"How was your morning, Haley?" Ginger asked as she stroked Boss' soft fur.

Haley stretched out on the settee—her beige pumps tossed to the floor—and pulled the pins from her curls. Her ponytail released from its faux bob. "It was good. Two autopsies under Dr. Gupta's tutelage. There were two other students present today."

"Sounds interesting, if not sad for their loved ones left behind."

"I try not to think about that part. I focus on the science," Haley said as she stifled a yawn. "Otherwise, I would likely go crazy."

"Well, we don't want that," Ginger said with a trace of humour. "We have enough craziness going on around here."

"For some reason, that makes me think about Louisa."

Ginger laughed. "Well, yes, there's Louisa. She's given up on Feathers & Flair."

"Already?"

Ginger nodded. "I wish I could pack her up in a trunk myself and ship her back to her mother. That sounds unloving of me, doesn't it?"

Haley chuckled. "It sounds *sane* of you."

"I'm astonished that Sally is so keen to get her back."

"There's no accounting for a mother's love."

"Dear me," Ginger said with a grin, "we sound cruel."

"You're right," Haley said. "Let's change the subject. How did your enquiries go yesterday? I'm sorry I couldn't assist. Who did you end up seeing?"

"Miss Blythe and Mr. Piper. I confess to visiting Miss Blythe with the intention of talking her out of the wedding."

"I sense a 'but'."

"Well, I failed on that account, but there was just something not quite right about her. When she first started spending time with Oliver, she was happy, more relaxed. Now she seems really wound up about something, something more than just her forthcoming nuptials."

"Guilt?" Haley said. "Do you think she pushed Mr. Edwards over the rail?"

"Perhaps he'd been giving her unwanted attention, maybe threatening to stop the wedding."

"Why would he do that?" Haley said. "Surely not to have her to himself. The fact that he was a married man notwithstanding, there are plenty of young girls to prey on."

"Predators like that can become obsessive, I believe."

Haley conceded. "That's true. Especially if what they desire becomes out of reach. A mentally unstable person might not even desire the object until it's unavailable to them."

Ginger casually stroked Boss' forehead as she considered Haley's words. "It could explain why Mary's mood had altered so much recently. She was quite determined to go through with the wedding, and if Mr. Edwards was a problem. . ."

"It comes down to intent at this point," Haley said. "Was it an impulse attack, or did she plan ahead?"

"Mary knew the schedule, and she was suspiciously late."

"Definitely a suspect," Haley said. "Up there with Miss Howard and Miss Bertram, who also had reasons to remove Mr. Edwards from this earth. Tell me about Mr. Piper."

Ginger sipped her tea and let out a long breath. There

was no getting around telling Haley about Basil being there.

"Now isn't that a coincidence?" Haley said wryly.

"It was! There was no way he could've known I was going to be at the mental hospital at that time. Otherwise I would've accused him of following me."

"Except that he was there first."

"Except for that."

"Was he useful, at least?"

"His identification papers got us past the gatekeeper, where I would've surely been turned away."

Haley nodded in approval.

"Mr. Piper reluctantly revealed that Miss Catherine Edwards was once an inmate there."

Haley's dark eyes widened with interest. "For what condition?"

"Melancholia."

"Thankfully, there've been some advancements in treatments for the mentally infirm," Haley said. "I'm afraid former treatments could be quite barbaric."

"Something happened to cause Catherine Edwards to beg her brother to discharge her. Apparently, she'd been doing quite well until that point. A painful treatment, perhaps?"

"Likely. Poor thing. It might not be a good idea for her to be home alone."

"I'll get Felicia and Louisa to pop in to see her," Ginger said. "They need something worthwhile to do."

"Two peas in a pod, those ones," Haley said.

"Basil thinks Mrs. Edwards is guilty."

"Then why go to the trouble of interviewing everyone?"

Ginger smirked. "In case he's wrong. He wouldn't want me to uncover that fact, now, would he?"

"So, you'll continue your tandem investigation?"

"It would seem so."

"You don't find it too awkward?" Haley asked. "Just yesterday you could barely mention his name without turning red as a beet."

"That's not true!"

"It is!"

"Well, I was fine in his presence today. We were friendly."

Haley's brow shot up. "Friendly?"

"Yes, *friendly*. I suppose you could say we are friends again. But that's all we're to be," Ginger insisted. "As you know, I'm walking out with Captain Beale."

"Yes, but you're not in love with him."

"I know. That's why I can trust him with my heart. He can't break it."

Haley stared at Ginger over the rim of her crystal glass. "If you say so."

Ginger roused Boss awake and put him on the floor. He stretched and trotted over to his bed beside the hearth which was still orange with a small fire.

"I need to get ready for tonight's gala at the Ritz. Are you sure you don't want to come?"

Haley snorted. "And face the judgmental glares of the snooty upper-upper class? I'd rather perform an autopsy on myself. Besides, I'm exhausted."

# CHAPTER NINETEEN

*L*ords and ladies—sirs and honorables, barons, dukes and even a prince—were present at the high society gala event at the Ritz Hotel. The ornate room had a multitude of electric chandeliers hanging from high ceilings trimmed in gold moulding. Gentlemen in tailored black suits, crisp white shirts, and black bow ties, and ladies in sparkly gowns and lavish jewellery swirled around the marble dance floor. Potted palm trees flanked the impressive stage now occupied by a nine-piece string and brass band playing the latest in jazz, waltz, and blues.

This was a world far removed from the one Ginger was acquainted with at St. George's Church. The parishioners there were commoners, unrefined, and for the most part undereducated. Her friendship with Oliver was the conduit responsible for folding her life into the lives of the poorer classes—a result of her concern for Scout Elliot, now her ward, when he was living like an orphan on the streets. Ginger admitted that her life felt richer now for having known Oliver and the people in his care.

Ambrosia, Felicia, and Louisa were in their glory, dressed in the latest fashions straight from the racks of Feathers & Flair.

William extended his hand to Ginger in his offer to take to the dance floor. "Shall we?"

Ginger accepted with a sincere smile. William looked dashing in his black suit and tie, shiny leather shoes, and with his face freshly shaven. A recent haircut had even managed to control his waves.

Ginger wore a sheer, emerald-green, crepe de chine sleeveless evening gown, loose fitting over a shorter green rayon slip. Her long white gloves reached her elbows, and her headpiece sparkled. Together she knew they were a striking pair.

William was a fair dancer. Not quite as natural as Basil —but she mustn't think of him. It would be terrifically unfair to William, who stared at her with unabashed admiration.

"How lucky am I to be dancing with the prettiest lady in the room?"

Ginger didn't even blush. She'd heard similar sentiments from other dance partners in the past. The compliment was hardly unique and was probably spoken tonight by many of the gentlemen in the room to their well-dressed dance partners.

"Perhaps I am the lucky one, Captain Beale," she returned.

Captain Beale led her in gracious circles around the ballroom. "Together we are the luckiest of them all."

They returned to their table when the dance ended in time to overhear the tail end of an ungenerous conversation.

"I heard she slurps her soup."

"I wouldn't doubt it. Perhaps she is adopted."

Haley had been right about there being snooty gossipers in the crowd; however, the judgements were coming from Ginger's own family!

"Felicia, about whom are you speaking?" Ginger asked, then she put up a palm. "No, don't tell me. I don't want to be guilty of defamation."

Ginger sipped her champagne, enjoying the tickle of the bubbles down her throat and the lightness it brought to her mood. She smiled at William, but his eyes had focused on something behind her, and whatever he saw caused a dark cloud to shroud his face.

"What is it?" Ginger asked as she turned in her chair, and then her heart stammered. "Oh."

Basil Reed looked dapper in his black suit ensemble: crisp white shirt, white satin waistcoat, and black bow tie. The lines around his eyes and mouth made him look mysterious and intriguing, and the bit of grey at his temples, distinguished. Ginger wasn't the only female in the room captivated by London's recent, most eligible bachelor. Every lady was staring, including those at her own table.

"Blimey," Felicia muttered.

"Language, Felicia!" Ambrosia chastised. "You are a lady."

"Well, isn't he just the bee's knees?" Louisa said dreamily. "If you don't want him, Ginger, can I have him?"

Ginger glared at her sister. "Don't be crass. Besides he's much too old for you."

Louisa sniffed. "No older than father was than mother."

*Oh, mercy.*

Ginger forced herself to look away. William reached for her hand and gripped it tightly.

"What on earth is he doing here?" he said seriously. "Isn't a police officer getting a bit above his station attending a gala like this?"

William sounded exactly like the haughty, judgmental people Haley had dismissed.

"Basil is a gentleman," Ginger explained. "His father is the Honourable Henry Reed."

"What's he doing at the Yard, then?" William said sounding incredulous.

"Basil was invalided out of the war early on. He felt that serving in the Metropolitan Police was a good way for him to do his bit, and he just stayed on."

"But *why?*"

"It makes him feel like he's contributing to society." Ginger's annoyance grew with William's insensitive questioning. "Is that so hard to understand?"

William sat back without answering and took a long pull of his gin and tonic.

The sensual classical notes of *Blue Rhapsody* began, and William turned to Ginger. "Another dance?"

She answered politely, "One cannot say no to Gershwin."

Ginger allowed William to lead her back to the dance floor. They'd barely made a turn when Ginger felt a tap on her shoulder.

"May I cut in?"

Basil Reed stood tall. His hands were clasped in front of him and his eyes longingly locked on Ginger.

"We've only just started, ol' chap," William said tersely.

"I'm asking the lady," Basil said without removing his gaze from her.

Ginger stammered. "I-it's all right William. We mustn't be rude. It's just one dance."

William's face turned an unappealing shade of red as he released Ginger's hand and stormed off the floor.

"I'm afraid I've created an unenviable situation for you," Basil said as he pulled Ginger close. His nearness was intoxicating, and her knees felt as if they had pooled with water.

"You did make quite an impression," she said. "I didn't think these kinds of events were of much interest to you."

"Yes, well, I've heard this is where the beautiful ladies could be found. I'm single now, as you know."

"I'm sure all of London knows it," Ginger said cheerlessly. *William* certainly was aware of it. "So why aren't you dancing with some of the other ladies?"

Basil's eyes were pools of emotion. "I think you know."

*Oh, mercy!*

Inhaling deeply, Ginger was determined not to allow Basil's charms to have an impact on her. A drastic change in subject was in order.

"Haley and I came up with a new theory regarding Miss Blythe. Like Miss Howard and Miss Bertram, Mary Blythe is young and pretty. And impressionable. Perhaps Theo Edwards had set his sights on her. It's possible he'd become obsessed, and perhaps had some ammunition with which to cause a scandal and interrupt her marriage to Oliver."

"It's an interesting theory," Basil said. "However, her marriage was prevented by Theo Edwards' death."

"Only temporarily," she answered. "It's being rescheduled."

"We can't forget Mr. Piper," Basil returned.

Ginger risked looking Basil straight in the eye. "Do you think an obsession by Mr. Piper with Mrs. Edwards is more likely?"

Basil spun Ginger around. "I think Mrs. Edwards' guilt in the matter is more likely. Humiliated women have been murdering their husbands throughout time."

"Yes, but poison is usually more to their liking," Ginger said. "This murder is quite physical."

"Which takes us back to Mr. Piper."

"Yes, I suppose you're right."

Ginger allowed herself to relax into Basil's lead, appreciating how enjoyable it was to dance with someone at his level of skill. Her mind went back to the last time they'd danced together in the sitting room of Basil's townhouse. They'd dance to Isham Jones'

"Swinging Down the Lane," cheek to cheek, hearts beating wildly as one. They'd declared their love for one another.

She'd just given him a gift—the Waterhouse painting of *The Mermaid*, which had, for years, hung above the mantel of the fireplace in the sitting room at Hartigan House. Its value went beyond its financial worth into the sentimental. It was a gesture she'd come to regret, and the space above the hearth still remained empty.

Their bodies moved in time to the music, effortlessly, as if they were one and not two. They stared at each other without speaking, the whole affair feeling intensely intimate. Ginger noticed that other dancers and those standing on the edges or seated at the tables had started to watch. What Ginger and Basil had on the dance floor felt whimsical and magical.

Until William strode across the room like the navy captain that he was and broke the spell.

"I'm cutting in, Mr. Reed," he stated, bringing the couple to a standstill. "Ginger, allow me to finish the dance."

"William, don't be silly. You're making a scene."

"*I'm* making a scene? Everyone is watching *you*. And even if I am," William added indignantly, "I feel it's my right to."

"Captain Beale," Basil said. "Lady Gold has made her desire known. We shall finish the dance."

"Since you're not moving your feet, I'd say, you've already finished."

Basil answered coolly, "I say we're not."

William stood nose to nose with Basil, his fists clenched at his side. "Shall we take this outside?"

Ginger couldn't believe it. "William!"

William ignored her. "As men. Not as captain or chief inspector."

Basil remained calm. "If you like."

Ginger returned to her table to collect her things with as much dignity as she could muster. Never in her life had she been the object of such a juvenile fight of words for her attention, and she wasn't about to wait around to watch words come to fists. As it was, the gossipers tittered. She should've taken her cues from Haley and stayed at home.

# CHAPTER TWENTY

"A few, we hear, add up." Ginger sipped her breakfast tea as she read aloud the crossword puzzle clue from the Boston newspaper she subscribed to. It came several days late, but Ginger liked to keep abreast of what was going on in her American hometown. Haley appreciated the updates as well.

"Sum," Haley said as she bit into a croissant.

"What are you two talking about?" Felicia said. She arrived to breakfast wearing her silk oriental house gown, a habit Ambrosia deeply frowned upon. Perhaps since she'd just spooned hot porridge into her mouth, Ambrosia kept her opinion to herself.

"It's a play on words," Ginger explained. "A few equals 'some,' and when you add numerical values together you get the three-letter homonym, 'sum.'"

Felicia's eyebrows furrowed together. "Too early in the morning for me to care."

"It's almost nine," Ginger shot back.

Louisa dragged herself in with a yawn and helped herself to the bounty cooked earlier by Mrs. Beasley. "Weren't you a lump of coal last night?" she said to Ginger. "Leaving early, *and* in a very impolite manner, I might add."

"It's the ongoing saga between Ginger and Basil," Felicia said between mouthfuls of scrambled egg. "Will they or won't they?"

"Felicia!" Ginger said with abhorrence.

"It's true. I for one wish you'd just make up your mind and get on with it. It's getting tiresome."

"Pick William, and leave Basil for me," Louisa said.

Ginger snapped the newspaper dramatically before folding it closed. "That's Captain Beale and Chief Inspector Reed to you."

Ambrosia patted her mouth with a cotton napkin. "For once I agree with Felicia. It's very unbecoming of you to lead both of them on."

"I'm not leading anyone on!" Ginger turned to Haley. "Please, do come to my defence."

Haley wisely shook her head. "Nope. I consider myself intelligent enough to stay out of the Gold family matters, especially when it comes to matters of the heart."

"Sometimes I despise you," Ginger said with a grin.

"Sometimes you *envy* me," Haley countered.

"Truer words have not been spoken." Ginger sipped her tea then asked Haley, "I'm going to visit Catherine Edwards after this. Would you like to come with me?"

"Actually, I can. My shift today doesn't start until noon."

"Perfect."

Boss was outside with Scout going for the dog's morning constitutional, so Ginger popped into the kitchen to let Lizzie know she was leaving soon. "I'm afraid I can't take Boss with me."

"That's fine, madam. I'm happy to look after the little chap for you."

"Thank you, Lizzie."

Ginger really didn't like to leave Boss at home so much, but when she was working on a difficult case, she often didn't have the choice. Lizzie had proven to be not only an excellent lady's maid, but also a good chaperone for Boss and Scout.

GINGER MOTORED through the streets of London like an old pro. At least *she* thought so. Haley sat stiffly in the passenger seat, and Ginger gave her credit for not criticising her driving skills for once, though by the look on her friend's face, one would think she smelled bad fish.

Haley's colour returned when Ginger pulled to a stop in front of the Edwards' home. "What is it that you hope to find out?"

"I'm not sure," Ginger said. "Her explanation for her time spent at the mental hospital."

Ginger used the knocker on the door of their brick house. After a lengthy wait, Ginger thought that perhaps Catherine wasn't at home, but then the lock clicked, and the door opened.

Catherine Edwards stood on the other side looking

much thinner than Ginger remembered. Obviously, the girl wasn't cooking for herself. Ginger made a mental note to ask Mrs. Beasley to prepare a dinner basket and get Lizzie or Grace to deliver it.

"Hello, Miss Edwards," Ginger started pleasantly. "How are you?"

"All right, I guess."

"Miss Higgins and I thought we might come in for a visit. Would that be to your liking?"

Catherine shrugged then opened the door wider, allowing Ginger and Haley to step inside.

The late spring sun had risen brightly that morning, making it hard to adjust one's eyes to the dim interior. Ginger suspected that the curtains hadn't been opened since the day Esme Edwards had been arrested, nor the house cleaned or dusted in that time.

Catherine headed to a chair that had a number of empty glasses on a small table next to it. She lifted up a ball of fine yellow wool stabbed with a knitting needle left on the seat before sitting.

Ginger and Haley sat on either end of a short sofa. A wooden grandfather clock across from the hearth ticked loudly.

"Would you mind terribly if I drew back the curtains?" Ginger asked.

Catherine glanced up from her knitting, her brow furrowing as if the thought hadn't occurred to her.

"Yes. That would be nice."

Ginger pushed open the old velvet panels and held in the urge to cough as a tornado of dust filtered through the sun's rays. She unhooked the latch on the window and pushed it open.

"There," she said, returning to her spot on the sofa. "Fresh air and sunshine. Does our health a world of good."

Catherine nodded mutely, her eyes remaining focused on her creation.

In normal situations, the hostess would offer the guests some tea. Ginger shrugged at Haley. Perhaps this was a role usually taken on by Esme, and the thought hadn't even occurred to Catherine.

"How are you managing on your own, Miss Edwards?" Ginger asked.

"I'm very lonely. And very sad."

"I can imagine," Haley said. "Losing your brother in such a tragic manner and then to have your sister-in-law taken away."

Catherine dropped her knitting. "Yes. I'm alone."

"Would you like some company?" Ginger asked. "I could arrange for a companion."

"No, thank you. I don't want a stranger here. Esme wouldn't like it either."

"Very well. But if you ever need anything, you'll let someone know? The reverend or Mrs. Davies, perhaps?"

Catherine kept her eyes on her knitting. "All right."

"Again, we're so sorry that this has happened to your family," Ginger began. "I don't mean to be insensitive, but can I ask, do you think your sister-in-law did it?"

Catherine hesitated then nodded. "She hated my brother."

"Why is that, do you think?" Haley asked.

"Because he didn't love her the way he loved me."

Ginger felt a sense of alarm. Had Theo Edwards violated his own sister? She broached the subject gently. "Did your brother ever do anything to you to make you feel uncomfortable?"

"What do you mean?"

"Did he say or do things, like touch you . . . inappropriately, like a husband would with his wife."

Catherine screwed up her face. "No! Why would you say such a terrible thing? Theo was the best brother in the whole world!"

"I'm sorry," Ginger said, wondering if Catherine was—as Shakespeare was famous for saying—protesting a little too much. "I didn't mean to offend."

Haley shifted forward in her chair. "We know you spent time at the County Mental Hospital. Did something happen there that made you want to leave?"

Catherine burst into tears, and Haley grimaced at Ginger as if to say, "Oops, and, now what?"

Ginger went to Catherine and patted her on the shoulder. "There, there now. Everything is going to be all right." She handed the weeping girl her handkerchief.

"Is it?" Catherine said. "They're going to send me back to that horrible place. I just know it."

Catherine opened the handkerchief and blew into it. "I'll kill myself before I let them put me back there."

"Oh, Miss Edwards," Ginger said, thoroughly disturbed by Catherine's words. "Don't say such a thing. Your brother's killer shall be found out, and justice shall be done. I promise you'll be all right."

Catherine bounded into Ginger's arms, nearly knocking her over. "Oh, thank you, Lady Gold."

Haley left the room and returned shortly with a glass of water. "Drink this, Miss Edwards," she said. "You'll feel better."

"Thank you." Catherine sipped the water and added the glass to the group of empty ones on the occasional table. She picked up her knitting.

"What are you making?" Ginger asked.

"Baby booties. For the baby."

Haley raised a questioning brow. Surely, Catherine wasn't with child?

"Whose baby?" Ginger asked softly.

"Mary Blythe's. She's going to be a mother, didn't you know?"

# CHAPTER TWENTY-ONE

"What are you going to do now?" Haley asked as she and Ginger returned to the Crossley.

"I need to revisit Mary Blythe and ask her if Miss Edwards' allegations are true."

"That should be an interesting conversation," Haley said. "From what I observed, Catherine Edwards isn't exactly mentally stable."

"Do you think she's fibbing?"

Haley lifted a shoulder as she considered Ginger's question. "It's possible. Then again, the insane are often the most honest." Checking her wristwatch, she added, "I'm afraid I can't join you. I'm due back at the hospital."

"Would you like a lift?"

Haley grinned as a bus approached. "I wouldn't want to keep you from your case."

Ginger watched as Haley disappeared onto the red wooden bus filled with strangers looking out at her. The lumbering vehicle moved slowly with the traffic, sure to stop many times before reaching Haley's destination. Ginger couldn't understand why her friend preferred that to a quick ride in the Crossley.

As Ginger drove towards the Blythe residence, her mind raced. Was Mary indeed with child? And was it possible that Oliver was the father? She couldn't imagine this type of indiscretion of her friend, but anything was possible. Was that the real reason he'd agreed to a quick wedding ceremony? It would explain why he wasn't willing to end the engagement, other than a matter of keeping his word.

Mary Blythe was just leaving her house when Ginger pulled up and parked in front of it.

"Miss Blythe," Ginger called as she exited her motorcar.

Mary Blythe turned, and a frown formed on her face. "I'm quite busy at the moment, Lady Gold," she said. "I've got errands to run."

"That's fine," Ginger said, catching up. "I'll walk with you."

Wearing a cotton floral-print day dress and sturdy pumps, Mary held her handbag close to her chest as she kept her quick pace along the pavement. She wore a wide-brimmed hat pulled low to shade her eyes from the sun, or perhaps, Ginger thought, to keep from having to look people in the eye.

"How are you?" Ginger asked. "Are you holding up?"

"So long as the police have the killer and justice is done," Mary said in a clipped tone.

"Do you believe Mrs. Edwards to be guilty?"

Mary spared a glance in Ginger's direction. "Isn't she?"

"It hasn't been proven by a jury as yet."

Mary slowed as she pondered Ginger's point. "But if not her, who else?"

A motorcar rumbled by with a large black dog panting out of the back window. It barked in greeting. The distraction allowed Ginger to avoid answering the question.

Moments later, Mary stopped at a red cast iron Royal Mail cylindrical pillar box embossed with a gold crown and the letters GR on its side. She riffled through her handbag and removed some envelopes.

"Wedding invitations with the new date," she explained. "I might as well just give you yours."

"Miss Blythe," Ginger started. "I have a rather delicate question to ask you, and I wouldn't if such a serious case wasn't at hand."

Mary held out an envelope with Lady Gold written as the recipient. "Very well."

"Are you in the family way?"

Mary's cheeks turned cherry red, and her hands began to tremble. She pressed the collection of envelopes to her chest in an attempt to calm them. "Why would you ask me such a thing? Oliver would never . . ."

*Oliver would never.*

"Miss Blythe, am I to *assume* the answer to my question?"

The rosiness of Mary's complexion drained to white.

Her brown eyes filled with tears, and try as she might, lips quivering, she was unable to hold in her sobs.

"Oh, Lady Gold!"

Mary produced a handkerchief and cried silently into it, her thin shoulders shaking.

"Miss Blythe," Ginger said gently. "You're in a serious situation, and I'd like to help."

Mary dabbed her nose and stared back with bloodshot eyes. "How can you help? Everything is ruined now. All because of Theo!"

Ginger was quick to notice her use of Mr. Edwards' Christian name, and her heart dropped. "Was Theo Edwards the father?" she asked.

Mary nodded, her expression pinched in emotional torment. "He lied to me. I feel so foolish." She took a moment to daintily blow her nose. "I felt so powerful and alive when I was with him. Naïve enough to believe that I was the only one. I was seduced, Lady Gold. I was weak and I'll never forgive myself."

"So, you found yourself in this unenviable position and the only answer was a quick wedding."

Mary nodded, not having the decency to look ashamed. "Oliver made it so easy. The rumour was that he was in search for a wife. I took what I'd learned from my time with Theo. Oliver was quite willing to speed up the process, with a little . . . encouragement."

Ginger could only imagine, in Mary's desperate state, how she might've teased and seduced Oliver to get what she wanted.

"So, now you're the liar," Ginger said.

Mary swallowed. "Yes."

Wiping her face dry, Mary stared at her bundle of invitations before returning them to her handbag. "How did you figure it out?" she said with a tone of resignation. Her palm pressed against a slightly rounded stomach that was still easily hidden.

"Catherine Edwards," Ginger said.

"Oh, yes. She came across us once, when Theo and I were arguing. She must've overheard. I'm actually shocked she didn't spill our secret sooner." Mary straightened her slumped shoulders and waited for a horse and carriage to continue by before asking, "Are you going to tell Oliver?"

"Don't you think you should do it?" Ginger replied.

Mary shook her head. "I can't. It's too humiliating. Please, will you do it for me?"

"Of course," Ginger said. She'd rather Mary did it, but it wouldn't be fair to Oliver to allow him to continue without knowing the truth.

Mary glanced about, avoiding direct eye contact with Ginger. "I'm damaged goods now. I'll have to run away."

"There are homes in place that are designed to help women in your predicament."

Mary sighed. "I know about them. Homes for ruined women."

Ginger only nodded. She'd helped Matilda Hanson who'd found herself in a similar crisis, and brought her to Hartigan House for her confinement, but she couldn't make that same offer to Mary Blythe. Miss Blythe had lied to Oliver. Almost tricked him into a marriage intending to pass off another man's child as his. That was unforgivable.

"Miss Blythe, did you kill Theo Edwards?"

Mary stilled. "I confess I'd dreamed about it, but it wasn't me. I didn't kill him, but I'm glad he's dead." She spun on her heels and practically ran away from Ginger and back to her house, hat brim down and handkerchief pressed to her face.

# CHAPTER TWENTY-TWO

Ginger felt ill. Not only did she have to tell her good friend that his fiancée had been deceitful, but also, Mary Blythe had just jumped to the top of the suspect list. She needed to let Basil know about her conversation with Miss Blythe, but first, she had to speak to Oliver.

A dark bank of clouds had rolled in, seemingly out of nowhere, and drops of rain tap-danced on her windscreen. She turned on the wipers to a rather unpleasant scraping sound, but they moved the water so she could see more clearly.

Feeling a sense of urgency, Ginger pressed down on the accelerator. Unfortunately, she didn't spot the puddle that had gathered in a pothole, and the stream of water that flew up and outwards when her tyre drove through it hit a passing pedestrian. The man, now drenched from the knees downward, raised a fist and shook it Ginger's way.

"Oops. Sorry, sir," she said without stopping. There was nothing much she could do about his damp trousers anyway.

Ginger pulled into the cobbled drive at St. George's Church and stared at the green Austin 7 in confusion. Basil Reed was here, but why? Had he got a break in the case?

She stepped out of her motorcar, retrieved a bright yellow umbrella from the back seat, and snapped it open above her head. Just as she started toward the tall wooden doors, Oliver and Basil stepped outside, Oliver hatless with a black umbrella and Basil with his trademark trilby on his head.

"Ginger!" Oliver said on seeing her. He approached with Basil on his heels.

"Hello, Oliver." Ginger's gaze shot to Basil. "Is everything all right?"

"I'm afraid the church has been vandalised," Oliver said with a mournful sigh. "Dreadful."

Ginger scanned the church exterior and saw nothing out of the ordinary. "Where?"

"This way," Oliver said. "I was just about to show Chief Inspector Reed."

"Hello," Basil said, now that Oliver had stopped talking.

"Hello," Ginger responded coolly. She hadn't forgotten the embarrassing spat Basil had got into with William the night before. "I didn't think vandalism concerned the Yard, but of course, with the murder inquiry . . ."

"Exactly," Basil said.

They rounded the corner, beyond the bed of irises, and Ginger's mouth fell open. "Oh, mercy."

Her favourite stained-glass window with Jesus and the saints was broken and the word, "Fornicator," painted onto the stone exterior.

"I have no idea who would do this or why they would write such a thing." Oliver stared woefully at Ginger. "I swear, I've been the perfect gentleman with Mary. We certainly haven't crossed any moral lines."

Thinking of Catherine, Ginger said, "Whoever did this is obviously not in their right mind."

"Mary can't see this. Our wedding is already marred by murder. Oh, dear, we'll have to postpone the wedding again."

"Oliver, why don't we see if Mrs. Davies could make us some tea," Ginger said, more for Oliver's sake than hers or Basil's. She couldn't remember ever seeing him so emotionally frayed.

"Good idea," Oliver said. "I'll do that." He turned on his heel and left Ginger and Basil staring at his back.

"Poor old chap," Basil said. "He's quite rattled."

"Indeed. So, what do you make of this?" Ginger wanted to keep their conversation civil and professional.

"Someone is upset, obviously. However, it's not necessarily connected to Theo Edwards' murder. It could be an unfortunate coincidence."

"What broke the windows?" Ginger asked. "Have you seen inside the sanctuary?"

"Yes, we'd just come from there." Basil pointed to the jagged rocks in the flower gardens. "A rock."

"It couldn't have been Esme Edwards," Ginger said, "being locked up."

"Actually, she was released last night. Not enough evidence to hold her."

Ginger blinked. Had Esme Edwards been in the house when Ginger had visited Catherine Edwards? Maybe she'd jumped to conclusions, presuming Catherine to be guilty.

"You could've mentioned that at the gala last night," she said tersely.

"I didn't know," Basil explained. "Morris made the decision after I'd gone home."

Superintendent Morris was a large man with a larger ego. Not one of Ginger's favourite people, she was quite certain Basil's boss had climbed the ranks to his position through a network of powerful people he knew rather than as a result of competent output on the job.

She huffed, barely concealing the annoyance she felt.

"Ginger, I feel I should apologise."

Ginger glanced up at him, his hazel eyes soft and imploring. A sudden urge to run a finger along that familiar jawline was so strong, she had to turn away.

"About your friend William, and how I behaved," Basil said. "It was uncouth of me."

Ginger swallowed before responding. "I appreciate your willingness to own up to your side." William had yet to do it, she thought ruefully.

"For a navy captain, he *is* rather sensitive."

Ginger shot Basil a disparaging look. "It's not an apology if you append it with criticism."

"Yes, you're right." Basil stepped under the church eaves to take shelter from the rain, which had increased in intensity. "How is the old chap?"

"Honestly, I wouldn't know." Ginger had refused to take his call over breakfast as she had still been too angry over what had transpired at the Ritz Hotel gala. She didn't like how possessive he was being. Perhaps, she should feel flattered, but instead, she'd grown annoyed.

Basil's eyes lingered on Ginger, and she quickly averted her gaze. She wasn't going to let him get under her skin.

"I've just come from visiting Mary Blythe," she said, eager to change the subject.

"Oh? I was going to go there from here. What did you learn?"

"She's in the family way."

Ginger felt a sense of smug satisfaction at the shock that registered on Basil's face. She'd been the one to uncover a vital fact. "And it's not Oliver's," she added. Basil's eyes narrowed as he considered the implications.

"Does Reverend Hill know?"

Ginger slowly shook her head. "No. It's why I came."

"Who's the father?"

Ginger raised a brow.

Basil guessed. "Theo Edwards?"

"Mary confessed it to me today."

"It explains the message on the wall," Basil said. "I wonder if Morris acted too rashly in releasing Mrs. Edwards."

"You know what they say about a woman scorned." Ginger said. "Although, Catherine—"

"Yes."

Ginger motioned to the vandalism. "She's the one who tipped me off."

"Esme Edwards or Catherine Edwards. Maybe they're in this together?"

"We can't dismiss Mary Blythe," Ginger said.

Basil nodded. "She's a clever girl. She could've done this to throw the scent off herself. It's a tactic tried by other criminals." Basil called over one of the constables who was scouring the area and taking notes, and gave him instructions to pick up Mary Blythe for questioning.

"Before she decides to do something like leave town," he said to Ginger. She nodded in agreement.

As they started back to their motorcars, Basil said, "I think I need to talk to Mrs. Edwards again. Would you like to join me?"

Ginger considered Basil's question. He didn't need Ginger to tag along, and William certainly wouldn't like it if she did. Was that why Basil had asked her? As a jab at Captain Beale? No. Basil had been including her on his interviews long before William had come on the scene. William needn't even know. Really, what business was it of the captain's anyway? With that thought, she'd made up her mind. "Yes. Would you give me a moment to speak to Oliver first?"

"I'll wait in my motorcar."

Ginger found Oliver inside having tea with Mrs. Davies in the kitchen.

"Hello, Lady Gold," Mrs. Davies said warmly. "Would you like a cup?"

A spot of hot tea would've been nice since the rain had come with a chill. "Thank you, but no. I'm afraid I can't stay long." To Oliver she added, "Could we have a word in private?"

They stepped into Oliver's office, and Oliver took his seat, threaded his fingers together, placed them on the desktop, and leaned in. "What's on your mind, Ginger?"

Ginger eased into one of the chairs facing him. "I'm afraid I have some rather distressing news."

"Dear Lord, not more. When it rains, it pours, does it not?"

"Apparently."

"What is it?"

"It has to do with Mary."

Oliver unlatched his fingers and leaned back. "Yes," he said cautiously.

"I've just come from a visit with her. It seems her desire to marry you wasn't exactly . . . honest."

His cheeks grew pink in anticipation of bad news. "Please, Ginger. Just say it."

"Very well. Mary is expecting."

"Expecting what?"

"A child."

Oliver's pale lashes blinked wildly. "That's not possible. We've—" The pink in his cheeks bloomed to crimson as understanding dawned. "Oh."

"I'm so sorry," Ginger said.

Oliver's expression crumpled. "That would explain her eagerness to wed quickly."

"I'm afraid it gets worse."

"Oh, dear."

"Theo Edwards was the father."

The silence between them grew so thick that Ginger could hear herself swallow.

Oliver pulled open his desk drawer and retrieved a half-empty bottle of whisky. He didn't bother to use a glass, just twisted off the top and took a swig.

"I do apologise," he said after wiping his mouth with his sleeve.

"Not necessary. I know how big a shock this must be."

"Yes. Very." He inhaled deeply and let out a long breath.

"You don't have to go through with the wedding now," Ginger said. "I know you had doubts."

"Yes, but what shall happen to her? To her child?"

"She can give it up for adoption. There's a more pressing problem than that."

"What?"

"She had motive, opportunity, and means."

The deep rose colour drained from Oliver's face. "No. She wouldn't have."

"We don't know that for sure. If Theo threatened her in any way, she might have been desperate enough to do it."

"But the vandalism—" Oliver's gaze dropped to his lap. "Oh dear—that's why that word was chosen." He looked up at Ginger. "Someone knew."

"I believe so."

"But if Mary was responsible for Mr. Edwards' death why would she write that?"

Ginger repeated Basil's theory. "To take the focus of the murder inquiry off her. It makes her look like the victim."

Oliver pushed his chair back, pinned his elbows on his thighs, and cradled his head in his hands. "This is a disaster."

Ginger went to his side and placed a hand on his shoulder. "It'll blow over in time, Oliver." She hoped her words provided some comfort to her friend. She hoped her words were true.

Once Oliver reassured her that he'd be all right, at least for now, Ginger joined Basil in the Austin.

"That was awful," she said as she collapsed her umbrella and closed the passenger door. "Poor man!"

Basil started the engine, but before he could put the gear into reverse, another police motorcar pulled up behind him. Basil rolled down his window.

"What is it, Constable?"

"A disturbance was called in from the home of Miss Mary Blythe. Miss Blythe has been found unconscious and bleeding."

# CHAPTER TWENTY-THREE

By the time Basil and Ginger arrived at the Blythe residence, police motorcars were blocking the way. Ginger's pulse jumped at the sight of the white ambulance with the letters LCC—London County Council— inscribed on the side, and its back double-doors opened wide. It meant that things were more serious than she'd hoped.

Basil raced through the pouring rain to the front door, and Ginger kept to his heels just barely staying dry under her umbrella.

"Chief Inspector," the constable said when he saw them. "Come this way."

Mrs. Blythe hurried over to Ginger when she saw her. The elder Blythe lady looked to have aged ten years since the last time Ginger had seen her—the skin on her face grey and sagging, her eyes brimming with tears, and her nose red. Ginger collapsed her umbrella before leaning it against the wall and extending her arms, taking both of Mrs. Blythe's cold hands in hers.

"Oh, Lady Gold, it's horrible. I was only out for an hour, two at the most, visiting Mrs. Barker, and when I got home. . ." Mrs. Blythe's lips began to tremble uncontrollably as she whispered, "I found her."

"Is Miss Blythe . . .?"

"She's alive, thank God, but bruised terribly. There's a lot of blood, though. I can't account for it."

Ginger called on the same constable who had greeted her and Basil at the door. "Would you take Mrs. Blythe into the kitchen and make her some tea?"

The constable nodded and guided Mrs. Blythe by the elbow.

Ginger joined Basil in Miss Blythe's bedroom and watched as the ambulance attendants moved Mary onto a stretcher.

"What happened?" Ginger asked. She had a sudden shot of remorse at having left Mary alone after she'd revealed her deceit. "Did she do this to herself?"

Basil shook his head. "No. She was attacked." He pointed to the candleholder on the floor, its end covered in blood. "She has bruising on the side of her face and, I'm afraid, on her abdomen."

Ginger hadn't noticed Mary's facial injury as it was on the side away from where Ginger stood. Mary's skin was a pasty white, her lips a pale blue, and her breath shallow. She looked close to death, and Ginger desperately hoped Mary would make it through this.

The doctor who'd responded to the call approached. "Am I free to go, Chief Inspector?"

"Yes, Doctor."

"I'll be at the Royal London Hospital if you need me."

"Doctor," Ginger asked before he could leave. "Did she lose the baby?" That would account for the blood loss.

The doctor frowned. "I'm afraid so."

*Oh, mercy.*

Once Mary was rolled out of the room, Sergeant Scott began to take photographs.

"The men shall bag the evidence once Scott is done," Basil said.

"Someone has to tell Oliver," Ginger said.

Basil nodded. "I'll get Sergeant Scott to go to him when he's finished here."

Ginger would go herself, but she'd come with Basil and didn't have her motorcar. Besides, she wanted to go with Basil to the next interview.

"Shall we call on Esme and Catherine Edwards?" she asked.

BASIL KNOCKED on the front door of the Edwards' residence, and like last time, the response was so slow that Ginger thought there mightn't be anyone at home. But unlike last time, it was Esme Edwards and not her sister-in-law, Catherine, who opened the door.

Mrs. Edwards snorted when she saw Basil and then settled her gaze on Ginger. "I expected you, Lady Gold, since you're supposed to be helping me," she said accusingly. She glared at Basil. "Not him."

"May we come in, Mrs. Edwards?" Basil asked.

"What for? I've done nothing since your officers released me except keep to my own business."

"We would just like a moment of your time," Basil said.

"And if I refuse?"

"We could always do it at the station."

Mrs. Edwards huffed. "Come in, then, if you must."

The chair Catherine had occupied when Ginger and Haley had visited earlier that day was empty, and Mrs. Edwards didn't sit in it. Instead, she chose an identical chair next to it. The small occasional table that separated the chairs was now clear of the glassware. Ginger and Basil seated themselves on the sofa.

"I hope you're not expecting tea," Mrs. Edwards said. She squeezed her sizeable backside into the armchair. "As this shall undoubtedly be a short visit."

"We'll be as brief as possible," Basil said.

"Lady Gold, you're still working for me, are you?"

"Yes, Mrs. Edwards. Your cooperation with Chief Inspector Reed will be helpful to me. I'm really working hard to find out who killed your husband."

Esme Edwards snorted in Basil's general direction. "Very well."

"Where is Miss Edwards?" Basil asked.

"Having a lie down in her room."

Basil glanced at Ginger before replying, "We'll need to speak to her as well."

"Shall I wake her?"

"In a moment. Let's chat together a bit first. Did you visit Miss Mary Blythe today?"

Esme's chin retreated. "What? No? Why would I do that?"

"She was attacked this afternoon," Ginger said. "Would you know anything about that?"

"What! Why would I? I have nothing to do with her."

"Can you tell me about your relationship with Mr. Cecil Piper?"

Mrs. Edwards blinked in confusion. "What? There's no *relationship* between me and him."

"Relationships don't need to be romantic," Ginger explained. "Would you call Mr. Piper a friend?"

Mrs. Edwards tensed. "An acquaintance at best."

"Is there any reason to believe that Mr. Piper might want your husband dead?" Ginger asked.

"I would say it should be the other way around."

"Why's that?" Basil said.

"Because of how Mr. Piper treated Catherine."

This wasn't the answer Ginger expected.

"What do you mean?" Basil asked. "What does Mr. Piper have to do with Catherine?"

Mrs. Edwards sighed. "I might as well tell you as your kind snoop and claw until you've found what you're looking for anyway. You might've noticed that Catherine is a bit slow and pouty. Like a dark cloud follows her everywhere. She acts as if rain hits her head alone during a storm. I said to Theo, the girl's just looking for attention, but he insisted that she had problems in the head. He went and admitted Catherine to that mental hospital. I told him not to, but Theo never listens to me."

Ginger and Basil nodded. This was information they already knew, so they waited for Mrs. Edwards to continue.

"Just like I said she would, Catherine got worse, not better. She hated all the staff there, especially, for some reason, Mr. Piper. He said that it was normal for patients to strike out at those that worked closest with them. I finally put my foot down and insisted that Theo bring Catherine home, but by then, the damage had been done. She has never been the same since."

"Do you think something happened to Catherine at the County Mental Hospital?" Ginger asked. It wasn't unheard of for female patients to be taken advantage of.

Mrs. Edwards swallowed. "Catherine claimed that someone *touched* her."

"You don't believe her?" Basil asked.

"Catherine doesn't know the truth from a lie, Chief Inspector. I can tell you this: she never bore a child."

"Intimate encounters don't always end with the conception of a child," Basil returned.

Mrs. Edwards' fleshy hand flew to her mouth. "Chief Inspector!"

"Had Catherine been violated?" Ginger asked gently.

"I really don't see what this has to do with anything."

"Was it Mr. Piper?" Ginger asked.

"He says no."

Ginger shared a knowing look with Basil. Mrs.

Edwards had just confirmed that Catherine had been taken advantage of.

"Did Mr. Piper say who might've abused Miss Edwards?" Basil asked.

"No," Mrs. Edwards' huffed. "He wasn't about to inform on his work colleagues. They stick up for one another."

"Would you fetch Miss Edwards for us, Mrs. Edwards?" Basil asked.

Mrs. Edwards let out a long sigh, making a point that Ginger and Basil were causing her a great inconvenience. She pushed on the arms of the chair and heaved herself out.

"Catherine has probably got rid of anything that could tie her to Miss Blythe's attack," Ginger said quietly once they were alone.

"Possibly. That doesn't mean we can't get her to confess."

To the murder of Mr. Edwards? Or the attempted murder of Miss Blythe? It was possible that Catherine could be guilty of the latter without being guilty of the former. Mr. Piper was still a candidate for that.

Mrs. Edwards returned alone. "Sorry, but she's not in her room."

Basil glanced at Ginger and then said, "But you said she was home."

"She was. She must've sneaked out when she heard your voices. I don't rightly blame her." She scowled pointedly. "No one likes to be harassed by the police."

Basil stood. "Would you mind if we took a look in

Catherine's room?" The expression on his face made it clear that he wasn't asking permission.

"That's an invasion of a lady's privacy," Mrs. Edwards said.

"I shall remind you that this is a murder inquiry, with the addition of attempted murder."

Mrs. Edwards grimaced in her defeat. Ginger joined Basil as the lady led them down a short, dark passageway. She opened a door with a sigh. "I don't know what you expect to find."

Catherine's bedroom had bright white walls with a cherry wood floor. The wooden furniture had rounded edges and was stained a pretty slate-blue. The single bed was made with a soft-pink quilt trimmed in wide floral lace. Matching curtains hung around a tall window.

On top of the dressers were piles of knitted baby things: booties, sweaters, blankets. A search in the drawers and the standing wardrobe revealed even more. Ginger found Catherine's apparent obsession somewhat disconcerting.

"She was knitting baby booties when Haley and I were here this morning," she said to Basil, keeping her voice low. "I have a feeling she wasn't knitting them for Mary as she claimed."

Esme Edwards watched nervously from her position at the door, her hands cupped together at her waist.

"Why has Catherine knitted so many baby things?" Ginger asked her.

"A spinster needs a hobby. No harm in it."

Leaning in close to Basil, Ginger whispered, "Perhaps

Catherine conceived during her time at the mental hospital, lost the baby, and was unable to cope with her loss."

"It could explain why Theo Edwards brought her home."

Ginger glanced at the door, relieved to see that Esme had finally left them alone. "Why would Mrs. Edwards deny it?"

"It's possible she doesn't know, if the baby was aborted or miscarried before Catherine returned."

"Why would Theo Edwards keep the secret? Why not expose who did it?"

"Perhaps he didn't know."

"Then why would Catherine keep it secret?"

Basil shrugged. "Her attacker could be holding something over her head. If news got out, it would ruin her reputation and the reputation of her family."

"Catherine had caught Mary and Theo arguing about the baby," Ginger added. "It's how Catherine discovered the truth about them."

"This all adds fuel to her motive," Basil said grimly. "Catherine loses her illegitimate baby, and then has to stand by whilst Mary has one. With Catherine's own brother."

Ginger ran fingers under Catherine's pillow as a matter of course and stilled when she touched something.

"An envelope," she said, waving it at Basil. She opened the flap and read.

*Esme,*
*It's too hard for me to carry on.*

> *Goodbye.*
> *Yours, Catherine.*

Ginger felt a sharp stab of worry. She turned to Basil. "We need to find her."

"Mrs. Edwards!" Basil called, almost bumping into the lady as she stepped into Catherine's room.

"Have you two not finished yet?"

Ginger passed her Catherine's note.

Esme Edwards eyed Ginger suspiciously. "What's this?"

"I found it under Catherine's pillow," Ginger explained.

The colour drained from Esme's cheeks as she read the note. She lowered herself onto the edge of the bed. "Oh, dear."

"Has Catherine tried to take her life before?" Ginger asked.

Esme swallowed and nodded. "Not for a few years, though. Theo thought she was cured."

"Please, Mrs. Edwards," Ginger pleaded. "It's vital that you tell us everything you know."

Esme sighed. "Catherine believes she is in love with Cecil Piper."

"In love?" Ginger asked. "Then why did she want to leave the hospital so badly?"

"Apparently, her advances towards him in the mental hospital were too much for Mr. Piper, and one fateful night he succumbed to her seduction. He admitted it to Theo and vowed to marry Catherine, and then she lost the child. When that happened, Theo reneged on his agreement to allow them to marry. He said that no one knew, and no one needed to know."

Ginger stared down at the broken lady with pity. "Mr. Edwards broke their engagement?"

"At first, yes, but Mr. Piper soon came to the conclusion that their separation was for the best, but Catherine wasn't so quick to let go. She got into the habit of taking Theo's motorcar without asking, just needed a drive to clear her head, she'd say—but I think she was sneaking time away with *him*."

"But I thought he wanted to end it," Basil said.

Esme scowled. "He didn't want to get *married*. That's a whole different bag of potatoes."

"In that case, I'm shocked that Mr. Edwards allowed Mr. Piper to join the choir," Ginger said. Was Mr. Piper's desire to join the choir more about being near Miss Edwards than singing?

Esme cocked her head. "Theo wasn't really in a position to judge, was he?"

Indeed, not, Ginger thought. "Has Catherine been holding out hope that Mr. Piper would marry her one day?"

"Like a dog with a bone. She and Theo had a big row about it. Theo said he'd never give her blessing to marry anyone, especially him. Deep down, Theo never really forgave Mr. Piper."

"But they could have wed without Mr. Edwards' approval," Ginger said, knowing the law itself wouldn't have got in the way.

"Mr. Piper is shamelessly leading our poor Catherine along."

Ginger glanced at Basil. Mr. Piper had just jumped to the top of the suspect list.

"When did this argument between Miss Edwards and Mr. Edwards take place?" Basil asked.

"It was the day before he died." Esme stopped suddenly, her eyes wide. "You don't think that—"

*Catherine is the killer?*

"Mrs. Edwards, it's important that we find your sister-in-law," Ginger said. "Do you have any idea where she may have gone?"

"To see Cecil Piper, most likely."

# CHAPTER TWENTY-FOUR

The weather had worsened during their time interviewing Mrs. Edwards. The sky was a menacing collage of dark greys, and the rain so heavy that Ginger feared her umbrella would refuse to hold up. Despite her best efforts, Ginger's Georgette silk and lace frock was quite damp by the time she slid into the passenger seat of Basil's motorcar.

The windscreen wipers on the Austin 7 laboured under the weight of the pounding storm—*thwack, swish, thwack*. The effort barely cleared visibility before it disappeared again.

"It hardly seems safe to drive," Ginger said.

"Only fools would be out in this weather," Basil muttered as he motored onto the road and headed west towards the mental hospital. Apparently, London was filled with fools, proved by the number of motorcars heading in both directions, their large headlamps like massive bug eyes, often the only thing one could make out in the dense fog.

Even though she could hardly see two feet ahead, Ginger's eyes focused intensely on the road, as if she could keep the Austin from driving off it with the strength of her will. She found she was holding her breath, her lungs protesting, and she finally exhaled. Inhaling, she forced herself to normalise her breathing.

"Who killed Theo Edwards?" Ginger said, having gained control of her nerves. "Catherine Edwards or Cecil Piper?"

Basil answered without taking his eyes off the road in front of him. "They could've been working together."

"Something doesn't make sense." Ginger gripped the ceiling handle tightly. "If they were two lovers separated by Theo Edwards, what's kept them apart now? With Theo dead, they could marry without hindrance. Why is Mr. Piper hiding his feelings?"

"Perhaps he's not," Basil said. "What if it's Miss Edwards who longs for that relationship, and Piper doesn't? It's the position Mrs. Edwards put forward. Catherine Edwards kills her brother because he's refusing to bless the romance that she wants, and now she's being rejected by Cecil Piper."

"What about Mary Blythe's attack?" Ginger asked. "There are many reasons why Catherine might do it—jealousy, anger, hatred—but I can't think of one reason why Mr. Piper would."

"He could've done it on Miss Edwards' behalf. We don't know how bewitched he is with her, if at all."

"If Catherine Edwards feels rejected by Mr. Piper," Ginger said, "his life might be in danger."

Despite the hazardous weather conditions, Basil pushed the accelerator to the floor. Ginger took hold of the ceiling handle with both hands now and muttered a prayer. The Austin fishtailed on the slippery asphalt.

"We'll not be much help if we die first!" Ginger said.

Basil released the pedal, and Ginger breathed in relief. Her thoughts went to Haley—she'd be white by now. And Haley thought Ginger's driving was bad!

Basil came up behind two slow-moving motorcars snaking along this narrow road on the outskirts of London. "We may not make it in time with this traffic."

Before Ginger could respond, a flash of bright light stunned them. Lightning ripped the sky, followed by the deafening roar of thunder. Basil slammed on the brakes as the motorcars ahead of them came to a sudden stop. Horns began to blow as a large tree, now charred and split in half, started its slow, crushing fall across the road.

"Turn around!" Ginger barely got the words out of her mouth before Basil made a sharp reversal of direction. He manoeuvred around other motorists who were stopped and staring with stunned gazes.

The urgency in Ginger's chest was crushing. They had to get to the County Mental Hospital to prevent a tragedy, but how were they going to do that with the main access road blocked?

"There's more than one way to get out of London," Basil said. He swerved past oncoming traffic and Ginger actually grabbed onto her hat. This must be the fear Haley felt, though in her case, irrationally. Still, Ginger vowed to drive more gently when her friend was in the motorcar.

The rain was coming down in sheets, making streams out of cobbled roads and rivers out of smooth ones. The Austin swerved sharply and jerked to a stop, nearly throwing Ginger against the window.

"Basil!"

"Bloody hell," Basil said. He opened the door into the rain and stared at the damage. The grimace on his face grew even more dire. "Blasted tyre is flat!"

Oh mercy! How were they going to get to Cecil Piper now?

The rivulets prevented Ginger from seeing what was beyond them outside. She prepared her umbrella, quickly rolled down the window and opened the umbrella outside.

"What do you see?" Basil said, stretching over to her side.

"There's a pasture. A cow. Some sheep. A horse tied to a fence."

*A horse.*

Ginger stared at Basil, her mind turning. "Do you ride?"

He nodded and started to leave.

"I'm coming," Ginger said.

"Can you ride bareback?"

"Can you?"

Mercifully the rain began to lift but the damage from the sudden downpour remained. Basil held her hand, pulling her through the muddy ditch to the fence. Another pair of Italian shoes, ruined!

It was times like this when Ginger thought that Coco Chanel and her controversial new designs for trousers for women made a lot of sense. As it was, Basil had to help her over the fence, and there was no denying the ripping sound that followed her when she landed on the other side. Oh well. The rain had already ruined her frock.

"What about the owner?" Ginger asked. They didn't have time to ask or to inform anyone.

"I'm commandeering it for police business," Basil said as he untethered the horse. He helped Ginger up and then hoisted himself on behind her.

Snapping the reins, Ginger prodded the flank of the beast with her heels. Basil held on as they took off down the lane, westward, towards the mental hospital. The rain pelted their faces like grains of sand. Ginger kept her head down—her hat brim pushed forward as much as possible for protection.

The urgency of the situation didn't keep Ginger from being *fully* aware of Basil Reed's body pressed up against hers. Not to mention how her frock was forced up scandalously about her thighs, as there was no possible way she could've ridden sidesaddle. Especially without the saddle.

Taking shortcuts, they galloped down narrow roads and trotted along the tracks. Finally, after what seemed like ages, they arrived. With the dark clouds pressing in and around the County Mental Hospital, the asylum appeared disturbingly eerie. A flash of sheet lightning brightened the sky, and for a split second, Ginger was keen to believe in the supernatural. Undoubtedly, this place was haunted.

She squeezed the horse's flanks and headed in, its horseshoes clopping noisily on the cobbled drive as he whinnied his protest. Animals had a sixth sense about danger, and Ginger wondered if they were riding into some kind of trap.

Unlike their last visit, the grounds were empty. The lights flickered with the next flash of lightning and faded to black. Ginger felt as if she had entered a sinister film. Would Cecil Piper pop out from behind a tree and kill her?

But it wasn't Cecil Piper that caused Ginger's blood to run cold. She had to wipe the rain from her eyes as she blinked back in horror. On the rooftop of the main building, with toes gripping the edge, stood a drenched and shaking Catherine Edwards.

She pointed. "Basil!"

He hopped off and helped her down, and they dashed to the entrance.

Cecil Piper, together with a few other staff members willing to submit themselves to the chilly rain, raced outside simultaneously. Their mouths dropped open as they stared up. "Catherine!" Mr. Piper shouted. "Do come down this instant!"

"Lady Gold?" Mr. Piper said when he registered who had joined them. "Chief Inspector Reed? What on earth?"

"Never mind that," Ginger said. "How do we get to the roof?"

Basil instructed the others before following Ginger and Cecil Piper inside. "Get a blanket and be prepared to catch her if she falls!"

Inside the gloomy building, gloomier still with the storm's early darkness and the absence of electricity, Cecil Piper produced a handheld torch, which created eerie shadows.

"What happened?" Ginger asked.

Cecil Piper opened a door revealing the staircase and spoke over his shoulder. "She arrived, again demanding that I marry her. It's a long story, one that I'm ashamed of."

"I assume you rejected her advances," Ginger said as she followed Cecil up the stairs. "And that's why she wants to take her life?"

"She's mentally ill, madam. She needs treatment and medication. Maybe now the government will step in and force the issue."

Ginger had thought she'd find Catherine threatening Cecil Piper's life not taking her own. When they reached the final door, Ginger was quite out of breath. She hoped she wasn't too late.

Cecil Piper wrestled with the latch and flung it open, and Ginger let out a small breath of relief when she saw Catherine Edwards' thin and soaked form standing there. The roof was flat, and Ginger carefully made her way towards the distraught lady.

"Ginger!" Basil protested.

"It has to be me, Basil. She won't talk to a man. I'm certain of it."

Basil relented but kept close enough to Ginger to grab her while keeping back enough as to not pose a threat to Catherine.

"Miss Edwards, do take a tiny step back," Ginger said gently. "Just so we can talk a little."

Catherine twisted her neck towards Ginger's voice, causing her to quiver. Ginger held her breath. *Please, don't fall!*

Catherine's arms went out instinctively to reset her balance, shocking her enough to bring her away from the edge. Ginger leaned over to get her breath, both in relief that Catherine hadn't fallen, and from racing up the dratted stairs!

"Go away," Catherine said feebly.

"I will, I promise." Ginger took a small step forward. "But let's have a short chat, shall we? Can you tell me what is distressing you so?"

"I have no one left to live for. Theo is gone. Cecil doesn't love me."

"You have Esme."

Catherine scoffed. "Esme does *not* love me. She despises me. If it weren't for Theo, she'd have turned me out on my ear years ago. I'm doing her a favour."

Ginger recalled how the two ladies had comforted each other after Theo Edwards had fallen.

"I don't think that's true. She's quite concerned about you."

"She's protecting her reputation, that's all."

"Would you like to speak to Reverend Hill?"

"He'd just tell me I'm going to hell."

"Reverend Hill is a very compassionate man. He might be able to give you something to hope for, to hang on to." With each word, Ginger shifted closer to Catherine.

"That's the thing, Lady Gold. I don't want to hope anymore. I don't want to *hang on*."

"You're a young lady, Miss Edwards," Ginger said. "With years of your life ahead of you. There are plenty of suitable, young men, available to meet."

"You know that's not true, Lady Gold. The Great War stole them all. I shall live and die alone."

"You're not alone, love. I'm here."

Catherine stared at Ginger, now barely an arm's-length away. "I killed him, you know."

Ginger was certain she knew who she was talking about, but a clear confession would be good. "Killed whom?"

"My brother, Theo. He robbed me of my happiness. He robbed Esme too, though I don't care about her. Who knows how many other young ladies Theo hurt. He was a bad man. I hit him with the organ pipe and pushed him. I wanted Esme to go to jail for it. Then they'd both have been gone, and Cecil and I could have had the house." She added mournfully, "We were to live happily ever after."

"We still can!" Cecil Piper had climbed onto the roof. Soaking wet, his balding head glossing in the rain, he pushed up on his spectacles which were steamed up by his breath, and Ginger doubted he could see. "Come down and we can talk about our future."

"You're a liar, Cecil!" Catherine yelled. "Theo was right about that. I killed him for us and you still didn't want me." She stepped backwards, one foot sliding off the edge. Lunging, Ginger grabbed Catherine's wrist just as Catherine toppled and jerked backwards, her wet boots slipping out from beneath her. Catherine dangled by the one hand that Ginger held. Ginger's body slipped with her.

"I've got you!" Basil gripped Ginger's legs and leaned back, grunting with the strain from the weight of the two women.

The rain made Ginger's grip slippery and bit by bit, she was losing hold. Then she screamed.

# CHAPTER TWENTY-FIVE

When Pippins announced that William Beale was waiting for Ginger in the sitting room, she was stunned to realise that two days had gone by without the captain ringing her or Ginger ringing him. So much had happened in such a short time.

The captain was standing when she entered, and she greeted him warmly with a kiss on either cheek.

"Hello, William. Please sit down. Would you like a drink?"

William sat on the edge of the settee, his elbows resting on his knees. "I'm fine for now. I have something to say, and I'd rather just do it, if you don't mind."

Ginger eased herself onto the spot beside the captain and clasped her hands on her lap. "All right."

"You'll remember, surely, that I promised to make another proposal two weeks after the last."

Boss strolled in and jumped onto Ginger's lap, perhaps sensing Ginger was in need of some moral support. She stroked his soft fur. "It hasn't been two weeks, already. Only five days."

"Yes, I know," William said. "The thing is, darling, I won't be making another offer."

Hand still on Boss' back, Ginger said, "I don't understand."

"I see the way you look at the chief inspector—"

Ginger's palm shot up in protest. "He has—"

"Please, Ginger," William said kindly. "I see the way you look at him. You've never once looked at me that way. It's quite obvious with whom you are in love."

"William—"

"Say no more. I'm sure you'll agree, in time, that this is for the best."

He lifted her hand to his lips and kissed it. "Goodbye, darling," he said after a moment of awkwardness. He patted Boss on the head. "I'll see myself out."


GINGER WAS STARING BLANKLY at the empty hearth when Haley found her a short while later. They didn't light the fire in the summer, which was a shame. Snapping and crackling flames had a way of adding warm light and charm to a room. Without it, it just seemed too quiet and gloomy.

"Was that Captain Beale I just saw leaving?" Haley asked.

"Yes, it was. He came to say goodbye."

Haley walked to the sideboard. "I think this calls for a drink."

"I couldn't agree more."

"You've had quite the week, finding *and* saving a man's murderer."

"Well, I didn't save her. She fell."

The large blanket Basil had instructed the male staff members to hold out did its job of saving Catherine Edwards' life, though it wasn't enough to keep the poor girl from injury. She suffered a broken arm and several ribs.

Catherine Edwards confessed to the murder of her brother—she'd followed him upstairs to the balcony when the other ladies had been traipsing to the loo, miraculously missing sight of one another, either taking a different route or being hidden behind one of the cubicle doors. Earlier in the week when the organ tuner had been around, Catherine had serendipitously come to the church with Esme Edwards, and "in a moment of brilliance" – her words—she'd remembered the loose pipes when the uncontrollable urge to kill her brother befell her. She also confessed to attacking Mary Blythe and vandalising the church.

Normally, Miss Edwards would have faced the noose, but hopefully, since mental illness was involved, the courts would extend grace. Basil was confident she'd be sent to Broadmoor—the high-security facility for the criminally insane.

"All the same," Haley said. "You solved a crime and got dumped in one fell swoop. It's bound to make your head spin a little." Haley handed Ginger a glass of brandy. She lifted hers in the air for a toast. "To new beginnings."

Ginger clinked her glass to her friend's and added, "New beginnings."

"Speaking of new beginnings," Haley started, "what about giving the chief inspector another chance?"

Ginger gawked at her friend. "I thought you weren't a fan."

"I've had a change of heart."

"But he *left*!"

"He'd suffered a traumatic loss, and I now believe he did the noble thing by removing himself from your life whilst he dealt with it. He's back now and stronger. He certainly has his eyes set on you. You'd have to be blind not to see it."

Ginger sipped her brandy as she contemplated. William had just left her for good, and oddly, Ginger felt no remorse. She wasn't truly right for William's temperament, and if she were honest, his wasn't satisfying for her.

Could she give Basil another chance? *Should she?*

Ginger hadn't even had a moment to consider it thoroughly when Pippins interrupted with a message for Haley that would prove to change their lives immeasurably.

# CHAPTER TWENTY-SIX

*H*aley was white as a ghost when she returned to the sitting room, and Ginger was immediately filled with alarm.

"Haley, what is it?"

"That was my mother. My Joe—" Haley's face tightened with grief. "He's been murdered."

"Oh no, Haley. I'm so sorry." Ginger hurried to her feet. "Do you know anything about it?"

Haley was the only girl after her older brothers Ben, Harvey, and Joe. Joe was the one closest in age to her, and, Haley had explained, was the one with whom she had the closest friendship. Her eyes welled with tears as she shook her head. "The police haven't any leads. Oh, Ginger, I have to go back to Boston."

Ginger lost her breath. Haley would leave London? Leave *her*?

*Oh mercy!* She could be so selfish at times!

"Of course, you must go to your family. Whatever you need, I'm here for you, Haley."

Haley's shoulders crumpled, and she sobbed into her handkerchief. Ginger wrapped her arms around her and just held her tight. Ginger was well acquainted with grief and knew that the journey to emotional healing for her friend would be long and varied.

Haley inhaled and let out a long shudder. "Thank you, Ginger. I'm going to let the school know."

"I hope I don't sound insensitive, but what about your studies?"

Haley sighed. "I can't think about that now."

Haley was *leaving*. Ginger felt stabbed in the heart. She'd grown accustomed to Haley's presence in her life, greatly enjoyed her company, and valued their friendship tremendously. She swallowed before saying, "Of course. I'll cover the cost of your voyage."

Haley looked up, her lower lip trembling. "Ginger, I can't ask that of you."

"You're not asking. I'm offering. It's my gift and the least I can do."

"Thank you," Haley said simply.

"When must you go?" Ginger asked.

"Right away. I should leave for Liverpool tonight and catch the SS *Rosa* in the morning."

Ginger closed her eyes and sighed. This was all happening so fast.

Felicia entered with a book in her hand. "I just passed Haley on the stairs. She didn't look well."

Ginger stared blankly into space and lowered herself

back into her chair. "She just received bad news from home."

Felicia claimed a spot on the settee. "Oh dear. What happened?"

"Her brother Joe has died."

"Who died?" Louisa entered in time to hear the last word.

Ginger sighed again, not feeling up to dealing with Louisa, but she couldn't very well ignore her.

"Haley's brother," she answered.

"You can't be serious?" Louisa sat on the edge of a chair opposite Ginger. "That's terrible. What happened?"

"I don't know the details," Ginger said. "Only that he's been murdered."

"Who's been murdered?" Ambrosia tapped her walking stick on the floor towards the chair Louisa had occupied. She narrowed her eyes at the young girl and Louisa had enough sense to give up her spot and tuck in beside Felicia. Ambrosia slowly lowered herself, leaning heavily on her walking stick.

Ginger held in the temptation to sigh aloud yet again. She reached for Boss, her ball of furry comfort, and held him tightly.

"Who's been murdered?" Ambrosia repeated.

"Haley's brother, Joe," Ginger explained. "In Boston."

Ambrosia had never taken to Haley, but her expression softened. Ginger's grandmother-in-law was no stranger to loss.

"How dreadful," Ambrosia finally said. "It's never easy to get that kind of news."

"What's she going to do?" Felicia asked.

"She's going back to Boston." Ginger stroked Boss' fur, almost desperately. "She's leaving for Liverpool today."

"Today?" Louisa said. "So soon!"

"Sometimes, life throws a curve ball." Ginger smiled to herself. Haley would've appreciated her use of a baseball analogy.

"That really is sad," Louisa commiserated. "You always think you'll have another chance to see the people you love."

Ginger, along with Felicia and Ambrosia, stared at the girl. Louisa was generally a flighty and shallow creature and not one to spout off meaningful sentiments.

"So true," Ginger said.

Louisa amazed the room further. "Perhaps I should go back with her."

"You mean, you want to leave for Boston today?" Ginger couldn't conceal her surprise. Louisa had been so adamant about her wish to stay in London. Her maid had only left a couple of days ago. However, Louisa was known to—as the Americans said—turn on a dime.

"Yes, why not?" Louisa stood. "I've seen everything I want to see here, and truthfully, I miss my mother." Just before she pranced through the sitting room door, she looked back and glared at Ginger. "Don't you dare tell her I said that."

Ginger wasn't about to argue with Louisa. Considering the state that Haley was in, Ginger was glad that she would have a travel companion to watch over her, even if that companion was her self-absorbed half-sister.

"That girl is a whirlwind," Ambrosia muttered.

Two hours later—after teary goodbyes—the taxicab arrived and spirited Haley and Louisa away. Ginger felt bereft at her loss. She swooped Boss into her arms, retired to her room, and cried into her pet's soft neck.

# CHAPTER TWENTY-SEVEN

The first few days without Haley were practically unbearable. Ginger busied herself at Feathers & Flair and spent more time with Scout and Goldmine when she was at home. She felt some relief when she received the telegrams—one from Louisa and the other from Haley—announcing that each of them had made it back to their Boston homes safely. Haley was at her family home on their farm outside Boston. Unfortunately, there had been no new advancements in finding Joe Higgins' murderer.

After a time, Felicia and Ambrosia's rather large personalities filled the voids left by Louisa and Haley. "Give it time," Ambrosia had said. "It won't be long before you find another stray to bring home."

Perhaps that would be proven true, but it hadn't happened yet. Ginger did think about Mary Blythe on occasion. Thankfully, she had made a full recovery after Catherine's attack on her, and only a handful had known about her being with child. Still, the broken engagement with Oliver Hill had given the gossipmongers a feast to feed on, and Mary quietly disappeared from life at St. George's.

A month had flown by ushering in a lovely July full of summer sun, which had brought to bloom beautiful plants like freesia, gerbera, lilacs, and roses giving off their individual fragrant scents. Ginger sat out on the stone veranda in the back garden, drinking tea and working on the latest crossword in the *Boston Daily Globe*. She'd already scoured the paper for news about Joe Higgins, but like always, there was nothing mentioned about him nor how he died.

Scout was playing ball with Boss on the piece of lawn. As Ginger watched them, she couldn't stop her lips from tugging up into a smile. Despite certain losses, she now had Scout, and though she wasn't officially his mother, she counted herself as the most appropriate person in the young lad's life to fill that role.

"I think I wore him out, missus," he exclaimed as he collapsed on the lawn out of breath.

Ginger laughed. "I'm not sure who wore whom out," she said, though Boss was sprawled out with his front paws out front, his back legs stretched behind, and his long pink tongue hanging out of the side of his mouth as he panted.

Lizzie burst onto the garden through the morning room doors with excitement flashing in her eyes.

"Madam, these came for you!" She handed Ginger a bouquet of fresh long-stemmed roses and a wrapped parcel, the size and shape of a book. Ginger searched the bouquet for a card but found nothing. "Did you see who it was?"

"A delivery boy, madam."

Ginger sniffed the roses, enjoying the sweet scent, before handing the bouquet back. "Would you mind putting these in a vase?"

Lizzie bobbed and then left the garden with the flowers in her hand. Ginger turned her attention to the package, carefully untying the string and removing the brown paper.

She gasped in delight. Simon & Schuster's newly published crossword puzzle book, complete with its own pencil! Ginger had never seen such a compilation before and believed this was the first of its kind. She ran a finger over the blue canvas cover with the words, *The Cross Word Puzzle Book*, cascading in black font.

"How marvellous!"

Ginger still didn't know the sender and opened the cover to the first page in hopes of a clue. It was there.

*Dear Ginger,*

*I wish you many days of danger-free puzzle solving. I've created a rudimentary one of my own. Please give it a try.*

*Yours, Basil*

A sunburst of joy exploded across her chest, and deep down she had to admit she was glad the gift-giver was Basil Reed. He knew how she enjoyed doing crosswords; she conceded that Basil Reed did indeed know her quite well.

In pencil, Basil had created a simple crossword puzzle made of five clues.

One across: Jekyll's alter ego
Two down: A common picnic area
Three down: London's theatre district
Four across: the snake
Five across: ride this golden horse

Ginger solved it immediately in her head and chuckled. Hyde, Park, West End, Serpentine, Goldmine.

Basil wanted her to meet him at the west end of the lake in Hyde Park known as the Serpentine, and she was to ride Goldmine.

How fun!

Usually, when Ginger went for a ride, she wore her standard riding clothes—a riding skirt, which was actually a wide-leg form of trousers, so she could ride astride, a growing trend by female riders that still garnered many frowns from onlookers. But today, she was going to be even more daring by wearing actual trousers intended for women—brown fine-tweed sport knickerbockers that ended at the knee. She paired these with a long-sleeved white blouse, a matching waistcoat, a red tie, long socks that ended above the knee, and a pair of suede riding shoes. To this, she added her brown felt hat.

Ginger smiled at her image in the stand-up mirror in her bedroom. She'd come a long way since her arrival in London a year ago. Born Georgia Hartigan, Ginger had been christened with her pet name by her mother because of her red hair.

"Where are you going?" Felicia asked when Ginger passed her in the hallway.

"I'm going for a ride on Goldmine," Ginger said happily, avoiding a direct response. "I don't know when I'll be back."

Scout helped her saddle up the golden gelding. Goldmine's flank shimmied in excitement. "Where are you and Goldmine off to, missus," Scout asked as he handed her the reins.

"Hyde Park. Just an easy ride today."

"Sounds lovely, missus." Scout patted Goldmine's neck affectionately.

Ginger squeezed her gelding with her thighs and tapped his flank with the heels of her boots. "Let's go, boy."

Ginger took her time riding from Kensington to Carriage Drive, through Kensington Gardens and east towards the adjoining Hyde Park. She didn't want Goldmine or herself to break into a sweat getting there. She allowed the sun's rays to stroke her face, and breathed deeply of the fresh mid-morning air.

Trotting along the banks of the Serpentine, Ginger scanned the horizon, looking for faces and body shapes that would become distinguishable as Basil Reed. Her mind took a moment to register it was him, riding on horseback.

She felt a smile stretch across her face. Basil was astride an auburn Arabian in a gorgeous leather saddle with bulging saddle bags attached. He looked assured and comfortable in dark blue cotton trousers, a crisp shirt, and a bowler hat.

"A horse looks good on you, Chief Inspector Reed. Or rather, you on it."

"And you as well."

They both smiled, Ginger remembering their last ride together. She couldn't very well see how he looked on a horse with him riding the same horse, sitting behind her. Basil must've been thinking the same thing.

"I rather liked your previous attire." His eyes twinkled and Ginger wagged a playful finger.

"You be good."

Basil chuckled as he cantered his mount to her side. "I'll make no promises."

"Nice gelding you have there, Chief Inspector. Where have you been hiding him?"

Basil patted the muscular side of the Arabian's neck. "This fellow belongs to my father."

"He's lovely."

"So are you, Lady Gold. Thank you for coming."

"Your gift was intriguing, and your offer compelling."

"Shall we ride?"

Ginger snapped her reins and fell into place at Basil's side.

It felt good—the ride relaxing, their conversation easy. It'd been more than a month since the Edwards' case, and since then they'd met on occasion, for dinner or for walks in the park. They'd discuss music, politics, and world events, quite animatedly at times. There were many moments when Basil surprised her with witty humour, making her laugh.

Basil pulled up on the reins when they reached a flat, private spot under a lime tree with bountiful deep green leaves.

"I thought we might enjoy a picnic," Basil said as he dismounted. He stepped over to Goldmine and offered his hand. Ginger, of course, could dismount without assistance, they both knew that, but she appreciated his gentlemanly offer and accepted.

"What, pray tell, are we to picnic on?" Ginger asked. Basil hadn't mentioned anything in his puzzle about bringing food.

"Not to worry," he said. "I've taken care of that."

Now Ginger knew what the saddlebags were for. She watched as he removed a tartan blanket and spread it out. He opened a tin with Scotch eggs, sausage rolls, and a salad. Reaching into the second saddlebag, he produced a bottle of red wine and two glasses.

"You have come prepared," she said.

Basil spread the picnic out on the blanket and motioned for her to sit next to him.

"This is lovely, Basil, though I'm not sure I can account for the occasion."

Basil opened the bottle of wine and poured two glasses, giving one to Ginger. It was rather early in the day to begin imbibing, but she went along with it.

"Then why don't I just get to it?" Basil asked. Suddenly, he looked nervous and let out a short breath. He reached into his pocket and removed a small, square, blue velvet box. Ginger felt her heart lodge in her throat. She forced a swallow. He wasn't . . . Was he?

"Georgia Hartigan Gold, Ginger—" He opened the box to reveal a sparkly diamond cluster ring. "Would you do me the honour of becoming my wife?"

Her chest heaved, and she struggled to breathe. "Emelia's only been dead for two months."

"But we were separated for two years. I know people shall talk, but I don't care. I want you to be my wife." Basil ducked his chin, "Ginger? I love you. Do you love me?"

"Yes." The word came out as if a feather had caught in her throat. She gave it a second try. "Yes! I do. I do love you, Basil Reed."

"So? Will you marry me?"

Ginger Gold loved Basil Reed, and Basil Reed loved her. This was the truth that resounded in her heart.

"Yes!" She threw herself into his arms, not caring that their wine spilled onto the grass. "Yes, I will marry you!"

# CHAPTER TWENTY-EIGHT

St. George's Church was electric with anticipation. Red roses and white lilies filled the nave of the church, and candles spoke of the love and romance that the imminent wedding vows were about to profess. Felicia played the organ with more delicacy and efficiency than poor Mrs. Edwards could ever have achieved.

Ginger glanced at the ring on her left hand, marvelling at its beauty and how the August morning summer rays cutting through the stained-glass windows caused it to glimmer and shine like a treasure chest of jewels. She smiled at Basil and squeezed his hand. The last month they'd shared together had been the happiest days Ginger had experienced since Daniel had passed away. He would want her to be happy, and Ginger believed he'd approve of Basil Reed.

*Mrs. Basil Reed.* In time, she'd forget about the *other* Mrs. Reed and wear the title as her own. She'd miss being Lady Gold, but it was indeed time for new beginnings.

"It's starting," she said excitedly as the melody changed to the commanding tone that signalled the beginning of the wedding march. The bride entered the threshold, and everyone stood.

Matilda Hanson was radiant in her ivory gown. Following current trends, the gown hung loosely over her shoulders with a satin dropped waist and the hem landing at her ankles giving a full view of her white satin pumps. A crown-like accessory sat on the top of her head and from it, a long lace veil cascaded to the floor in soft white pools.

Miss Hanson's father walked her down the aisle as the entrance music played. Oliver's face beamed with pride and admiration, and Ginger was filled with joy for her friends. *This* was the better match.

*Felix culpe.*

Matilda's personal trauma had led to her leaving medicine and taking up midwifery. Theo Edwards unfortunate demise had led to Oliver not getting trapped in what was sure to be an unhappy alliance. Today Oliver and Matilda staring at each other with giddy, unconditional, and passionate love made Ginger's heart soar.

Reverend Markham opened with an introduction about the purpose of marriage and God's will for it. "Love is the gift and love is the giver. Love is the gold that makes the day shine. Love forgets self to care for the other. Love changes life from water to wine."

The ceremony was beautiful. Oliver and Matilda

exchanged vows as their friends and family looked on. Ginger cast a glance at William who had returned to London to stand by his friend. He sat with a pleasant looking woman whose face radiated with adoration when she stared up at him. Ginger smiled, feeling pleased for the captain.

Missing, of course, was the Edwards family. Ginger wouldn't accept payment from Esme Edwards for the work she'd done for the poor lady. She'd become a hermit in recent weeks, refusing to leave her home. Ginger had visited her a couple of times, but Mrs. Edwards had made it clear she didn't want visitors.

The marriage register was signed and the happy couple knelt together for the final blessing before walking, hand in hand, down the aisle and out of the church doors as husband and wife.

Basil whispered in Ginger's ear. "We're next, and I can't wait."

His voice made shivers run up and down her spine. Their date was set for October. Basil had wanted it earlier, but his parents had convinced him to wait at least six months after Emelia's death to preserve propriety. Oliver had agreed to officiate. Ginger and Basil wanted to keep their wedding simple and small—definitely not a high-society event, much to Ambrosia's and Mr. and Mrs. Reed's chagrin. She and Basil had already made their honeymoon plans for Scotland. Ginger had been a young child the last time she'd been to the northern country. Her imagination had concocted plenty of fanciful stories after having viewed the moorlands, and the many ancient and abandoned castles.

It was Basil's choice to take the train rather than drive—a new, fast-travelling steam engine that ran from London to Edinburgh had recently been christened the Flying Scotsman—how extravagant!

Ginger certainly didn't mind, so long as she was with Basil. Every day with him by her side proved to be a glorious adventure, and travelling by rail would surely be an exciting experience.

Besides, what harm could befall them on a train?

* * *

**HEY, WHAT ABOUT THE WEDDING???**

Good news! You are invited!

For fans of Ginger Gold and Basil Reed - this is the wedding you've been waiting for! The bride and groom prepare for their big day and, of course, things don't go exactly as planned. Told from the alternating points of view of many of the beloved characters in the world of Ginger Gold, you'll find yourself holding your breath, anticipating that happy ever after.

*The Wedding of Ginger & Basil* a companion novella best enjoyed after book 7 (Murder at St. George's Church) in the Ginger Gold Mystery series.

This is a mystery, but not a murder mystery.


On AMAZON or read free on Kindle Unlimited!


## WHAT'S HAPPENING WITH HALEY HIGGINS?
### Haley has her own new series!

**Death by Rum Running...**


IT's the hot and humid East Coast summer of 1930 and five years since Dr. Haley Higgins' brother Joe was murdered. The case has grown cold. The Boston Police Department may have given up on finding Joe Higgins' killer, but Haley never will. She's serious and savvy and has what it takes to hold up under depressive times. At least she finds some satisfaction doing her part as the city pathologist's assistant in solving other crimes.

A man is found dead inside Boston's oldest tavern—a "tea and coffee" house since prohibition became law. Another in a string of deaths related to underground rum running.

Haley doesn't care for nosy reporters, and Samantha Hawke is no exception. Demanding and presumptuous, Haley tries to stay clear of the ambitious Sam Hawke, but it turns out they may just need each other to solve this case without becoming the next victims.

### DEATH BY RUM RUNNING...

When a man is found dead at the Bell in Hand Tavern on Union Street, pathologist Dr. Haley Higgins and investigative reporter Samantha Hawke are both working the case. They want the same thing ~ to catch a killer. Though they don't exactly trust each other, they'll have to work together if they want to solve this case before becoming the next victims.

A spin off from the acclaimed Ginger Gold Mystery series, this clever, feisty, depression-era whodunit readers call "serious and suspenseful" and "entertaining mystery series" will keep you turning pages until the surprising yet satisfying end.

Buy Death at the Tavern today
or read free on Kindle Unlimited.

### WHAT'S NEXT FOR GINGER GOLD?

Life goes on for Ginger after Haley's departure in MURDER ABOARD THE FLYING SCOTSMAN.

ONE MUST NOT LOSE **one's head.**

One blustery day in October of 1924, newlyweds Mr. and Mrs. Basil Reed travel aboard the recently christened Flying Scotsman, a high-speed steam engine train that travels from London to Edinburgh, for their honeymoon. With only one short stop at York, Ginger anticipates time with her new husband will fly by.

She's wrong. Something terrible has happened in the Royal Mail carriage which forces the train to stop dead in its tracks. There's been a death and Chief Inspector Reed has been asked to take investigate.

It's a uniquely disturbing murder and Ginger and Basil are eager to puzzle it out together. What do the first class passengers have to do with the dead man? With another crime shortly discovered, Ginger and Basil soon realize they're not dealing with a run-of-the-mill killer—they're dealing with a mastermind who's not done playing with them yet.

Buy on AMAZON or read free on Kindle Unlimited!

Introducing the GINGER GOLD'S BOOK CLUB!

In doing research for the fictional mental hospital found in *Murder at St. George's Church*, I came across this information about a certain asylum in Hanwell located eight miles west of Kensington.

*Aerial view of the hospital c. 1920*

It had all the makings of the asylum I had envisioned for this story. The size of a small town, yet a prison for the patients who institutionalised, often against their will. They were even called *inmates* in those days. The brick buildings were neglected during the Great War, and the same war left the country with a lack of finances to properly upkeep the hospital. The decay gives the sense of eeriness we often attribute to such places.

After I'd plotted the first draft and the ending scenes, I came across this tidbit. On 11 June 1910, nurse Hilda Elizabeth Wolsey followed a female patient who climbed one of the fire escapes and then along the guttering of the ward roof. She held on to the patient until help arrived - but unlike Ginger and Catherine Edwards - they were both lowered to the safety of the ground. For this act of heroism she was awarded the Albert Medal which was exchanged for a more suitable George Cross in 1971.

London County Mental Hospital was renamed Hanwell Mental Hospital in 1929 and again in 1938 to St. Bernard's Hospital. It was bombed during WW2 and by 1950, was no longer operational.

Find out more at these websites.

https://londonhistorians.wordpress.com/2013/08/26/the-hanwell-asylum/

https://en.wikipedia.org/wiki/Hanwell_Asylum

If you enjoyed reading *Murder at St. George's Church* please help others enjoy it too.

- **Recommend it:** Help others find the book by recommending it to friends, readers' groups, discussion boards and by suggesting it to your local library.
- **Review it:** Please tell other readers why you liked this book by reviewing it on Amazon or Goodreads.
- **Suggest it** to your local librarian.

**WHAT'S HAPPENING WITH HALEY HIGGINS?**
**Haley has her own new series!**

It's 1930 in Boston Massachusetts, and Dr. Haley Higgins is the assistant to the city coroner. Her brother's murder remains unsolved. She'll never stop trying to find his killer, but new strides in forensic medicine have helped her to solve other murders and she finds immense satisfaction in that.

Investigative reporter Samantha Hawke ~ byline Sam Hawke ~ is blond, beautiful and broke, no thanks to her no good husband who's been on the lam for a decade. Her position at the Boston Daily Record is more than a job ~ it's payback.

When a man is found dead at the Bell in Hand Tavern on Union Street, Haley and Samantha are both working the case. Haley's looking for justice and Samantha's after recognition and a raise. They may want the same thing ~ to catch a killer ~ but that doesn't mean they want to be friends.

**Death by Rum Running...**

When a man is found dead at the Bell in Hand Tavern on Union Street, pathologist Dr. Haley Higgins and investigative reporter Samantha Hawke are both working the case. They want the same thing ~ to catch a killer. Though they don't exactly trust each other, they'll have to work together if they want to solve this case before becoming the next victims.

A spin off from the acclaimed Ginger Gold Mystery series, this clever, feisty, depression-era whodunit readers call "serious and suspenseful" and "entertaining mystery series" will keep you turning pages until the surprising yet satisfying end.

www.leestraussbooks.com

## WHAT'S NEXT FOR GINGER GOLD?

Life goes on for Ginger after Haley's departure in MURDER ABOARD THE FLYING SCOTSMAN.

## Past, Present and . . . Murder

One blustery day in October of 1924, newlyweds Mr. and Mrs. Basil Reed travel aboard the recently christened Flying Scotsman, a high-speed steam engine train that travels from London to Edinburgh, for their honeymoon. With only one short stop at York, Ginger anticipates time with her new husband will fly by.

She's wrong. Something terrible has happened in the Royal Mail carriage which forces the train to stop dead in its tracks. There's been a death and Chief Inspector Reed has been asked to take investigate.

It's a uniquely disturbing murder and Ginger and Basil are eager to puzzle it out together. What do the first class passengers have to do with the dead man? With another crime shortly discovered, Ginger and Basil soon realize they're not dealing with a run-of-the-mill killer—they're dealing with a mastermind who's not done playing with them yet.

OCTOBER 2018

**HEY, WHAT ABOUT THE WEDDING???**
Good news! You are invited!

For fans of Ginger Gold and Basil Reed - this is the wedding you've been waiting for! The bride and groom prepare for their big day and, of course, things don't go exactly as planned. Told from the alternating points of view of many of the beloved characters in the world of Ginger Gold, you'll find yourself holding your breath, anticipating that happy ever after.

*The Wedding of Ginger & Basil* a companion novella best enjoyed after book 7 (Murder at St. George's Church) in the Ginger Gold Mystery series.

This is a mystery, but not a murder mystery.

## WAIT, THERE'S MORE

Sign up for Lee's readers list and gain access to Ginger Gold's private Journal. Find out about Ginger's life before the SS Rosa and how she became the woman she has. This is a fluid document that will cover her romance with her late husband Daniel, her time serving in the British secret service during World War One, and beyond. Includes a recipe for Dark Dutch Chocolate Cake!

http://www.leestraussbooks.com/gingergoldjournalsignup/

It begins: **July 31, 1912**

How fabulous that I found this Journal today, hidden in the bottom of my wardrobe. Good old Pippins, our English butler in London, gave it to me as a parting gift when Father whisked me away on our American adventure so he could marry Sally. Pips said it was for me to record my new adventures. I'm ashamed I never even penned one word before today. I think I was just too sad.

This old leather-bound journal takes me back to that emotional time. I had shed enough tears to fill the ocean and I remember telling Father dramatically that I was certain to cause flooding to match God's. At eight years old I was well-trained in my biblical studies, though, in retro-spect, I would say that I had probably bordered on heresy with my little tantrum.

The first week of my "adventure" was spent with a tummy ache and a number of embarrassing sessions that involved a bucket and Father holding back my long hair so I wouldn't soil it with vomit.

I certainly felt that I was being punished for some reason. Hartigan House—though large and sometimes lonely—was my home and Pips was my good friend. He often helped me to pass the time with games of I Spy and Xs and Os.

"Very good, Little Miss," he'd say with a twinkle in his blue eyes when I won, which I did often. I suspect now that our good butler wasn't beyond letting me win even when unmerited.

Father had got it into his silly head that I needed a mother, but I think the truth was he wanted a wife. Sally, a woman half my father's age, turned out to be a sufficient wife in the end, but I could never claim her as a mother.

Well, Pips, I'm sure you'd be happy to know that things turned out all right here in America.

http://www. leestraussbooks.com/gingergoldjournalsignup/

VISIT LA PLUME PRESS TO SEE FULL CATALOGUE

**www.laplumepress.com**

Volume 3

**HIGGINS & HAWKE MYSTERY SERIES**

(cozy 1930s historical)

*The 1930s meets Rizzoli & Isles in this friendship depression era cozy mystery series.*

Death at the Tavern

Death on the Tower

Death on Hanover

**A NURSERY RHYME MYSTERY SERIES(mystery/sci fi)**

*Marlow finds himself teamed up with intelligent and savvy Sage Farrell, a girl so far out of his league he feels blinded in her presence - literally - damned glasses! Together they work to find the identity of @gingerbreadman. Can they stop the killer before he strikes again?*

Gingerbread Man

Life Is but a Dream

Hickory Dickory Dock

Twinkle Little Star

**THE PERCEPTION TRILOGY (YA dystopian mystery)**

*Zoe Vanderveen is a GAP—a genetically altered person. She lives in the security of a walled city on prime water-front property along side other equally beautiful people with extended life spans. Her brother*

*Liam is missing. Noah Brody, a boy on the outside, is the only one who can help ~ but can she trust him?*

Perception

Volition

Contrition

**LIGHT & LOVE (sweet romance)**

*Set in the dazzling charm of Europe, follow Katja, Gabriella, Eva, Anna and Belle as they find strength, hope and love.*

Sing me a Love Song

Your Love is Sweet

In Light of Us

Lying in Starlight

**PLAYING WITH MATCHES (WW2 history/romance)**

*A sobering but hopeful journey about how one young Germany boy copes with the war and propaganda. Based on true events.*

A Piece of Blue String (companion short story)

THE CLOCKWISE COLLECTION (YA time travel romance)

*Casey Donovan has issues: hair, height and uncontrollable trips to the 19th century! And now this ~ she's accidentally taken Nate Mackenzie, the cutest boy in the school, back in time. Awkward.*

Clockwise

Clockwiser

Like Clockwork

Counter Clockwise

Clockwork Crazy

Clocked (companion novella)

<u>Standalones</u>

**As Elle Lee Strauss**

Seaweed

Love, Tink

Lee Strauss is a USA TODAY bestselling author of The Ginger Gold Mysteries series, The Higgins & Hawke Mystery series (cozy historical mysteries), A Nursery Rhyme Mystery series (mystery suspense), The Perception series (young adult dystopian), The Light & Love series (sweet romance), The Clockwise Collection (YA time travel romance), and young adult historical fiction with over a million books read. She has titles published in German, Spanish and Korean, and a growing audio library.

When Lee's not writing or reading she likes to cycle, hike, and play pickleball. She loves to drink caffè lattes and red wines in exotic places, and eat dark chocolate anywhere.

For more info on books by Lee Strauss and her social media links, visit leestraussbooks.com. To make sure you don't miss the next new release, be sure to sign up for her readers' list!

Did you know you can follow your favourite authors on Bookbub? If you subscribe to Bookbub — (and if you don't, why don't you? - They'll send you daily emails alerting you to sales and new releases on just the kind of books you like to read!) — follow me to make sure you don't miss the next Ginger Gold Mystery!

www.leestraussbooks.com
leestraussbooks@gmail.com

# MURDER ABOARD THE FLYING SCOTSMAN

"I feel like a gooseberry," Felicia Gold whimpered. "How daft of me to join you on your wedding journey."

"You and many others," Ginger returned with a smile.

Seated aboard the Flying Scotsman, England's fastest train, Felicia shifted her weight and crossed her legs. "I *could* move to another compartment. Or even another carriage. I don't mind second class."

"Don't be silly," Ginger said. She turned to the handsome gentleman who sat as close as he could. "Basil and I love having you, don't we, darling?"

Basil Reed's hazel eyes twinkled as he gazed into his new bride's beaming face. "Of course."

"Your gushing happiness is starting to make me feel sickly," Felicia said. "At least you'll only have to put up with me half of the way."

Ginger stroked the small Boston terrier curled on her lap. Boss, short for Boston, had been a gift from her father after the Great War. She'd returned to their Beacon Hill home from France without her late husband, Lord Daniel Gold, who had perished in battle. Boss snored softly and was quite unperturbed by the foreign surroundings on board the train.

Smiling at Felicia, Ginger asked, "Is Miss Dansby meeting you at York station?"

"Yes," Felicia answered. "And her fiancé, Mr. George Pierce. I'm very curious to meet him. Irene describes him in her letters like he's a god. Not a physical blemish or character flaw to be found."

Ginger laughed. "Must be love!" She patted Basil's arm.

Basil raised Ginger's hand and kissed it. "*You* are perfection itself, Mrs. Reed."

"Please stop!" Felicia moaned. "Or I just might have to throw myself out the window."

"If you must, please do so before the train starts moving," Basil said wryly.

Through the glass compartment door, Ginger caught sight of an elderly lady dressed in black apparel. Assisted by a stick-thin porter, she entered the carriage. She appeared trapped in the nineteenth century with her tight-fitting coat, her long, heavy skirt, and a boat of a hat pinned to white hair that was piled into a bun on the top of her head. Her face was concealed by a thick black veil.

Despite using a cane to assist her slow, stilted gait, the lady stood upright and was most obviously wearing a corset. Ginger had a fleeting thought of Ambrosia, Daniel's grandmother and Ginger's house companion. Had she not had the influence of the younger set in her life, Ambrosia would undoubtedly have continued to resemble this latest passenger. Unfortunately, Ambrosia's new liberties didn't make her any happier, and the perpetual scowl and overall distrust of "this wayward generation" remained.

The lady nodded at the empty upholstered seat beside Felicia and said in a rather husky voice to the lad assisting her, "This is far enough."

When the porter opened the door, she said to Felicia, "You don't mind, do you? I'd rather not walk more than necessary, and my seat is in the last compartment down the corridor."

Basil answered for them all. "You're welcome to join us."

The porter assisted the lady into the plush seat. "Such lovely polished teak and brass! And these velvet chairs are simply marvellous," she said. "Thank goodness someone had the brains to make the backs high enough to support one's neck. I'll warn you good people in advance; I might embarrass myself by falling asleep. At my age, one tends to nod off without intending to."

The whistle blew, and the green carriages of the Flying Scotsman slowly and laboriously inched forwards. Loud rhythmic clanking came from the steel wheels. Gears screeched in response. With each rotation, motion increased in speed. White plumes of steam gushed past the windows and blocked their view of King's Cross Station.

"I'm needed in Edinburgh, for a funeral," their new companion offered.

"I'm sorry," Ginger said. "Is it someone close?"

"No. I barely knew him. I just like going to funerals. I know it sounds morbid, but I do have a fascination with death. It's my age, you see."

Ginger shared a stunned look with Felicia. The lady was quite forthright and clearly dressed as one in mourning.

"I was at the hanging of Susan Newell, a year ago today," the elderly lady continued. "What a spectacle that was! The first woman to hang in Scotland in fifty years. She refused the white hood. Her eyes nearly . . ." She opened her gloved hand by her eye and mimicked an explosion. "It wasn't pretty, let me tell you."

*Oh, mercy.* Ginger had to bite her lip to keep from laughing. "A funeral should prove to be rather boring after that."

"Oh no. It's a double funeral. The man was *murdered*. By his wife. Then she took her own life. A big family scandal with a bundle of money involved. When I read about it in the paper, I knew I had to go."

Felicia's eyes widened with incredulity.

"Do forgive my rudeness," the lady said. "I'm Mrs. Simms."

"I'm L—" Ginger stopped herself in time. She'd almost introduced herself as Lady Gold, a title she'd given up when she'd married Basil. "I'm Mrs. Reed. This is my husband Chief Inspector Reed, and my sister-in-law, Miss Gold."

Mrs. Simms turned her head sharply towards Basil.

"Are the two of you acquainted?" Ginger asked looking

between them.

"No, no. I do apologise for staring," Mrs. Simms replied, tilting her veiled head towards Ginger. "Sometimes my mind goes blank, goes on a bit of a holiday. The lament of old age." Frowning at Basil she added, "A police officer you say?"

"Yes, madam."

"What takes you to Edinburgh, Chief Inspector? A case for Scotland Yard, I presume?"

Basil patted Ginger's gloved hand. "My wife and I are on our honeymoon."

"Oh, how marvellous. Congratulations," Mrs. Simms said, beaming. "I'm sure you'll have a lovely time. The highlands are splendid in the autumn season."

"I was there as a child," Ginger said, "but it's exciting to take the Flying Scotsman."

"Shaves off two hours," Mrs. Simms offered. "Such a difference, especially at my age. And I love travelling on something so new." She inhaled deeply. "Still smells like fresh paint and new fabric. It's yet to be blighted with bad experiences like death and derailment. Or a robbery. You might be too young to remember, but the world's first train robbery happened in England."

"You're referring to the Great Gold Robbery of 1855," Basil said.

"Yes, indeed. It was quite a sensation. I was a youngster at the time and impressionable. My village talked about little else for months."

Mrs. Simms didn't, as Ginger was beginning to fear, talk their ears off and had, in fact, fallen asleep as she'd predicted. Felicia lost herself in a mystery novel. Boss, a terrific sleeper as well, jerked on occasion. *The result of some adventurous dream,* Ginger thought with a grin. She was content to lean into Basil and watch the scenery.

Presently, the conductor stepped into the carriage and announced loudly, "First sitting for lunch."

Felicia put her book down. "I'd like to dine. I'm feeling rather peckish."

Ginger took a moment to examine her reflection in the window, patted her red bob, and reinforced the curled tips that rested below high cheekbones.

Mrs. Simms' head bobbed up. Ginger could barely make out her eyes behind the black veil except to notice that they had opened.

"What's happening?" Mrs. Simms' voice was pitched so low that Ginger thought to offer her a glass of water.

"It's first sitting for lunch," Ginger explained. "Would you care to join us?"

"I was having the most interesting dream. A dismembered body was floating alongside the train." She turned towards the window as if she expected to see such a gruesome sight and then ducked her chin. "If you don't mind, I think I'd rather fall back to sleep."

In the dining car, Felicia confessed, "This will sound snooty, but I'm glad Mrs. Simms didn't join us. I dare say, her mind is frightfully *alarming.*"

FIND ON *MURDER Aboard the Flying Scotsman* on Amazon or request it from your favorite bookstore.